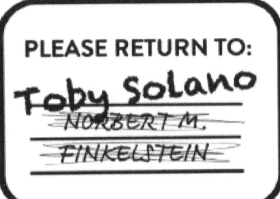

PLEASE RETURN TO:

Toby Solano

~~NORBERT M.~~

~~FINKELSTEIN~~

BY: FRANK MORELLI

ILLUSTRATED BY ALEXANDRA FREY

"While you're holding your breath or shaking your head at Toby Solano's impulsive actions, you'll fall in love with the tender heart that beats underneath his teenage bravado. A funny, poignant, intensely readable book!"

—Ann Campanella, author of Motherhood: Lost and Found and a founding member of AlzAuthors

"No matter your age, you can't help but smile at the middle school life of one Toby 'El Machina' Solano.
Thanks to the clever story-telling of Frank Morelli, you soon realize that young Toby is just a boy who wants to fit in and you find yourself cheering wholeheartedly for 'El Machina' to win his place in the world."

—Landis Wade, author of *The Christmas Redemption: A Courtroom Adventure* and host of *Charlotte Readers Podcast*

"Good books contain great characters who tell great stories while teaching valuable life lessons. Morelli delivers all three in his second book in the middle school 'Finklestein' series. *Please Return to: Toby Solano* is sure to please audiences of all ages!"

—**Mary Ann Drummond, author of *Grandma and Me*, *Meet Me Where I Am*, and *I Choose to Remember***

"What was there to like about the mischievous wrestling know-it-all new kid, Toby Solano? His cheeky, resourceful and courageous efforts at managing life in a new place and a new school never cease to entertain and amuse. Hilarious, spirited and relatable for kids in middle school."

—**Kathryn Harrison, author of *Weeds in Nana's Garden***

PLEASE RETURN TO:

~~Toby Solano~~
~~NORBERT M.~~
~~FINKELSTEIN~~

BY: FRANK MORELLI
ILLUSTRATED BY ALEXANDRA FREY

INtense Publications
www.intensepublications.com

INtense Publications

Paperback ISBN-13: 978-1-947796-48-5

PLEASE RETURN TO: Toby Solano

Contact@INtensePublications.com.

This is a work of fiction. Names, characters, places and incidents are either the product of the author's imagination or are used fictitiously and any resemblance to actual persons, living or dead, business establishments, events or locales is entirely coincidental.

This edition published by arrangement with INtense Publications LLC. The opinions expressed by the author are not necessarily those of INtense Publications LLC.

Cover and Book Design by Kassi Snider with Kassi Jean Formatting and Design

Illustrations by Alexandra Frey

www.INtensePublications.com

Printed in U.S.A.

For Luna and my favorite new "kid" in town.

Monday, January 7

I DON'T KNOW WHAT I did to end up in this town. In Mapleton. At least a million miles away from home in El Paso, Texas. Where I mattered. Where I could snap my fingers and get my math homework done for me or squint my eyes down tight and give another kid one of those stares that says, "Get your butt out of my seat before I pile drive you." And the kid would scram. Or wet his pants and keep the seat.

But here in Mapleton I'm anything but king. I'm barely a speck of dust on an old box of nonsense you have stored deep in the back of the attic where you'll never notice it or find another use for it again. I'm like the invisible man, which is weird because I'm hard to miss. I'm more like the invisible blob, oozing outside the hems of my t-shirt and over the bounds of my desk/chair combo as I sit in the back of Mr.

Finkelstein's class and give a little grunt when he calls out 'Toby Solano'. And when he ticks off the box for 'present' next to my name it's the only real evidence of my existence in this town. Well, other than this stupid journal. I just started writing in it today, so now there's a paper trail.

I got the idea about two weeks ago, even though I didn't know it at the time. That's when the moving trucks pulled away from the curb and kicked up something ratty and torn at the edges, and it was covered in grease from getting kicked around the street so many times.

Mom was on the phone with her real estate agent, so she didn't notice me smuggle a disgusting piece of garbage into my new room. And Dad? Well, he didn't notice because he's not here and I doubt he ever will be. It's not like I can blame him, because Mapleton's a dump and it's filled with the most annoying people on the face of the planet. At least that's what I learned in the journal I found. Because that's what it turned out to be. The mysterious object, I mean.

It wasn't an ordinary journal, either. It was written by the most bizarre and ridiculous teacher who's ever lived. And I read it. That's right, I read every last word because that's what you do when you move to a new town and it's just you and your mom and you have no friends and you find a weird journal. You can't blame me for that.

But all I learned was what I already knew when Mom said, "We're here!" and I looked through the windshield and the first thing I saw was an orange, highway cone. A common obstacle in the middle of the roadway. Not a cactus or a longhorn steer or the open Texas sky stretched wide above us. Nope. It was a highway cone, set up strategically between me and my real life. Between me and my dad. Between me and mattering.

At least that's what Finkelstein's little diary told me. 'Warned me' is probably a more accurate way of saying it, because that's where I learned about sniveling crybabies like Jimmy Baker and know-it-alls like Maya Providence. It's where I found out about the Mort-tician, possibly the crappiest wrestler of all time with an even dumber name. If I didn't spend my first two weeks in Mapleton laughing at the fools on the pages of Finkelstein's journal, I'd be forced to admit I completely wasted my holiday break sulking around in my new room.

Imagine my surprise last week when Mom and I showed up at Mapleton Middle School for our first days (she's a teacher, by the way) and I found out the same fools I'd been reading about are my new classmates. And the biggest buffoon of them all--Norbert M. Finklestein--is my new teacher.

Today was only my fourth full school day in this dumpster fire and, if anything, I've found the Jimmy Bakers and the Derek Meeks and the Mandy Mallomars of the world to be at least twenty times more insufferable than they appeared on the pages of my teacher's journal. For one, they're so focused on their petty, little lives they don't have a spare second to say 'hello' to the new kid in town. Like I'm some over-inflated ghost with spiky, black hair that passes directly through walls and their attention spans with the same level of detection. None.

On top of that, they're all a bunch of kiss-ups to their lord and savior, Mr. Finkelstein. Each and every one of them. They think the Mort-tician is some kind of intergalactic wrestling superstar, but I've got news for them. I climbed out my bedroom window last week and caught a few bouts of the MWF down at Mapleton Auditorium, and it's not exactly what I'd call 'wrestling at the highest level' even if the cheesy banner outside the event would lead you to believe so.

I mean, I'm surprised most of these two-bit wrestlers in Mapleton are allowed to own a driver's license, let alone take to the ring to battle it out in one of the world's oldest and most revered sports. And the Final Nap? Ha! No pun intended, but my Dad wouldn't be caught dead trying to perform the Mort-tician's wimpy, finishing move.

That's because my dad is a *luchador.* To put

it simply, he's a real wrestler. If you want a better definition (see: a longer one), a *luchador* is a traditional Mexican wrestler who fights in the *Lucha Libre* style, which means my dad kicks your butt with a brutal combination of high-flying kicks, slams, and acrobatic aerial stunts from the top rope. And he wears a *mascara*. A mask. It hides his true identity from all his screaming fans, and it's flashy and loaded down with all kinds of cool designs. My dad's *mascara* is so much tougher than that stupid piece of fabric that covers Mr. Finkelstein's face in the ring.

Maybe it's because my dad's a much better wrestler. A professional. Or at least he used to be until he destroyed his knee in a match and got stripped of all his belts and then told me one night he had to go back to Mexico City. "To get right," he told me. But I knew what he meant.

He needed focus. He needed to simplify his life. He needed to get as far from me and Mom as he could if he ever wanted to be Carlos "El Carisma" Solano again.

That's the last I heard from him. It's also about the time I landed Mom and me in this wasteland they call Mapleton. See, I may have been a little less than honest when I started this entry by saying I don't know what I did to end up in this town. I know *exactly* what I did. You tend to know that kind of stuff when the principal at your school sits you down and tells you you're expelled for hanging a kid up by his gym shorts in the locker room. I mean, how was I supposed to know he'd get locked in overnight? And how was I supposed to know his parents would raise a big stink about it? I mean, I got away with all the other pranks I pulled on people at that school and my classmates kind of liked my style. Or at least they never had the guts to say anything to me or anyone else about it without the fear of a pudgy, Texas fist slamming them between the eyes.

I guess it's hard not to know what landed you in a town after your mom gets called down to the same principal's office on the same day and he tells her, "Cait, I think it's best if you end your tenure with the school at the same time as your son's." So, Dad was gone. I was kicked out of school, and Mom had been locked out of her classroom. There was nothing left, so I guess Mapleton was a logical next step.

Now that we've been here a few weeks, I don't know how I'm going to outlast my boredom. I don't know how I'm going to survive being alone--without my dad and my friends at my old school. Without so much as another soul to notice I exist enough to purposely mispronounce my name as "Tubby" instead of Toby the way they used to do in El Paso before Dad taught me a few of his most fearsome wrestling moves. At least that would be an improvement over not existing at all.

For now I'll simply exist on the pages of this journal, an even better journal than that wimpy diary Mr. Finkelstein left stranded in the middle of my street. And I'll use it to collect all the evidence I need to prove how ridiculous the people of Mapleton are, and to convince Mom we need to move back to El Paso as soon as possible.

Wednesday, January 9

SEVEN GRUELING DAYS AT Mapleton Middle and I still feel like a space alien. And I still hate it here. I mean, my only friend is my mom (how sad is that?), there's not one restaurant in town that serves Texas brisket (okay, that may be sadder), and I've yet to have a single classmate set their tray down next to mine at the lunch table (nope, there's nothing more sad than a young man drinking chocolate milk alone).

Maybe the only thing worse is having to sit through Dweebie von Finkelstein's class each day after reading about these dimwits for my entire holiday break. Big mistake.

Take today's moronic class for example. Mr. Finkelstein had assigned *The Adventures of Tom Sawyer*, written by some riverboat captain named Mark Twain. I honestly don't know about the 'riverboat captain' stuff because I kind of jumped into the class midstream and I haven't caught up to the rest of my classmates. That means I haven't read the assignments I was supposed to read. The most I can tell you about Mark Twain is he had a pretty sweet mustache and that Tom Sawyer, his character, was a little bit like me. Misunderstood. A prankster.

Well, Mr. Universe (that's Finkelstein) split the class into two groups and set them off on different tasks, or what he called 'challenges'. The biggest challenge for me was keeping my eyelids from flapping shut and my nose from doing that weird grumbling, whistley sound it makes right before I'm out cold.

Next thing I know, the whole class springs into motion like the finely tuned sprockets inside an old machine. Like the ones you see down at the science museum. The only part that doesn't function properly, that doesn't fit in quite right with the other cogs and gears of the classroom is the spiky-haired, half-asleep boulder glued to his desk at the center of the chaos. Yep. Me.

I mean, Finkel-fart asked me if I wanted to be in Group A or Group B, but what did he expect? That I'd want to pal around with a bunch of creeps who never bothered to ask my name or sit with me at the lunch table? And did he want me to plaster a fake smile under my rosy cheeks and talk about a book I've never read with a bunch of strangers I never asked to meet?

Wasn't gonna happen.

So I sat back and observed. Like one does. And it wasn't pretty.

Good, old Finkel-face set Group A around a table by the window and told them to pretend they were Tom Sawyer trying to write a love poem to Becky Thatcher (I guess that's his boo or something?). Only they had to write the poems in some secret, Japanese format he called Haiku--which meant it had three lines with five syllables, then seven syllables, and then five syllables on those lines. They also had to start the poem with "My Dearest Becky," which happens to have five syllables. Trust me, I checked. That doesn't mean the whole thing wasn't stupid. Just not as stupid as the poems these bozos cranked out. I really mean it. I think poetry itself may have died a little today.

Like Mandy Mallomar's poem. I don't know what she was thinking when she rose from her chair and spouted off some nonsense like:

My dearest Becky,
You are important to me.
I think I love ye.

And then you had Derek Meeks. My goodness! That fool stood up and said something ridiculous, like:

My dearest Becky,
Do you happen to like me?
Please check 'yes' or 'no'.

About the only poem that didn't make me want to flat-out vomit was Maya's. I mean, she sounded kind of stupid. Just not totally stupid when she said:

My dearest Becky,
I wish you could see the good
Hiding in my heart.

And then there was Group B. The brilliant strategist (cough, cough), Mr. Finkelstein, handed each of its group members a handkerchief and a blindfold. Then he started moving all the furniture around the room, like the middle of class was the perfect time to audition for an interior design show. He handed one blindfolded member of the group--one Jimmy "Pitsniffer" Baker-- a ten-foot length of twine and told him to lead the rest of the group through the cave (whatever that means), making sure to leave a line behind them to map a path.

As an innocent bystander (and one who's never read a word of *The Adventures of Tom Sawyer*), this seemed to be the most ridiculous and least educational task in the history of modern schooling. But then Jimmy started to lead the troops through the random maze of overturned desks and stacks of textbooks, and I truly learned the meaning of the word 'ridiculous'.

First, Jimmy crashed face-first into the cinderblock wall under the white board ledge, causing each of his team members to literally 'head' 'butt' each other as they crawled in a single file line. That got a few laughs from the members of Group A. And from me. But then Jimmy Pitnsiffer tried to rally his troops and set them back on course, which resulted in a great, wriggling heap of arms and legs piled up at the head of the class--and tangled in ten feet of twine. That got a few more laughs.

But the finale of the piece was when all of Jimmy's team members stood up and took hold of the rope. That's when they confronted the largest and most fearsome obstacle they'd faced yet. And it sat in a desk at the center of the room just minding its own business, trying to stay clear of the stupidity.

They circled this obstacle not once, not twice, but five times--so confused were they in their blindfolded state at the obstacle's magnificence. But then came the sixth rotation, and the rope tightened. The members of Group B circled in closer and closer to the core of the obstacle. This young man. This boy named Toby Solano.

That's when the members of Group A burst out in laughter, and the members of Group B ripped off their blindfolds to reveal the errant path of their rope map. I didn't say a word, because I didn't think it was funny to be turned into a mummified boulder all wrapped up in their flimsy twine. I thought it was stupid.

I decided it was time to ask Mr. Finkelstein for a bathroom break. But then Coach Seam popped his head in the door and asked to make an important announcement, so I put my bathroom plans on hold.

The classroom fell silent and Coach Seam said, "The official wrestling season may have come to an end, but we thought you might miss the competition." I looked over in time to see Pitsniffer's eyes sparkling like a four-year-old's on Christmas morning. What a dweeb! "That's why," Coach Seam continued, "Mapleton Middle will sponsor a team in the district exhibition league that takes place over the spring." By now, Pitsniffer was so fired up I thought his shoes might turn into tiny rocket boosters and he'd lift off into space. "Signups will take place in my office between now and the end of next week," Seam said, and he popped back out the door as quickly as he'd come.

I mean, I'm not as obvious as Jimmy or anything (because that would be lame), but I have to admit skipping my bathroom break in favor of Coach Seam's wrestling announcement may have been the most exciting thing to happen to me since I moved to this ridiculous excuse for a town.

I don't know if I'll sign up. I probably won't. But if I did, I'd show all these small town nobodies what it means to be a wrestler. Especially the Mort-tician...the biggest nobody in the barrel.

Sunday, January 13

MY GOD. IS THERE a single thing about Mapleton that isn't terrible? First, I get slapped upside the head by its people, then by its food (some Texas BBQ? Some ribs?? A fish taco??? ANYTHING???), and now by its weather? Even Mother Nature's kind of lame here. It's always cold. Or dreary. Or both. It's nothing like El Paso, where the sun can melt a lizard fast to a rock before noon, and where the streets smell like eucalyptus and cactus flowers. Here, in Mapleton, the streets smell like dried leaves and stale acorns, and the cold keeps me burrowed deep down in my room for days on end, learning all the pointless dance moves from my favorite computer game, *Quadrant*. Blasting newbs all day in my room used to be enough to harden me for just about anything. Now it comes nowhere close to saving me from another week in Pointlessville, USA.

At least in El Paso I was sort of happy. At least I had Dad, and he'd take me down to Valenti's Gym where he'd slip the silver-trimmed *mascara* over his head and go to work on his training. And I'd watch and learn about flying *tornillos* and the lethal piledriver move which was once banned in all of wrestling. Sometimes Dad would remove the mask and he'd just be Dad again instead of "El Carisma", and he'd teach me how to punch the speed bag with the perfect rhythm--not too fast, but fast enough. Sometimes we'd roll under the turnbuckle onto the canvas and Dad would catapult me off the far ropes, and when I came springing back, he'd lift me high over his head and hold me there. Suspended. Like I was as light as a cloud.

We'd come home and Mom would have a batch of *chilaquiles* waiting for us. Dad would eat with a bag of ice on both shoulders and a knee, and I would eat with my homework sprawled halfway across the table, and Mom would eat while she graded papers in her lap and wrote lesson plans for the next day in her head.

And we were happy.

Even when I went to school, when the doors swung open and people saw Toby Solano, the sea of students in the hallways would part out of respect. And because none of them wanted the underwear bands twisted up over their heads super-atomic wedgie style later that day. It wasn't perfect, but it worked for me. I had it all mapped out in El Paso.

And we were happy. All of us.

Then Dad blew his knee to smithereens in that match and he had to leave town, and everything started to fall apart.

It made me angry. I mean, didn't my opinion matter? Couldn't anyone hear me? I guess that's why I did it. Why I let my anger ride shotgun and got Mom and I shipped out to Mapleton State Pen, aka, Mapleton Middle School. That's why I cornered Marty Wagner in the locker room and hung him from a hook by the seat of his pants. I did it out of anger, because it's not like the Wagner kid ever did anything to me. He was a pretty quiet guy, but when he disappeared for twenty-four hours without a trace and then made a surprise entrance dangling from his locker like a pinata, he spoke out loudly against one Toby "El Machina" Solano--which is totally unrelated, but I hope will be my wrestling identity someday, long after everyone forgets the time I may have crossed too far over the line of being a prankster, which I guess some people might just call 'being a bully'.

Still, I would have gladly stuck around in El Paso and faced the heat (and the warm weather, too) if it meant I'd never have to learn of the existence of Mapleton Middle School, or of this stupid town, or of Norbert M. Finkelstein.

And just as I was writing that last line, wouldn't you know it? The phone rang. I didn't pay much attention because Mom's kind of busy with the new house and, as far as I can tell, she's been the most popular person in Mapleton since we moved in. But then Ms. Popular stormed into my room a few seconds later and the place below her nose that's usually reserved for a pleasant, reassuring smile was replaced with  something that looked more like a lightning bolt. And her ears were somehow pasted back like an angry alley cat's and I swear there were literal sparks surging from the tips of each strand of her straight, black hair.

She walked right in and yanked the cord on my *Quadrant* session. Before I could push a complaint past my lips she pounced on me with, "That was your English teacher!" and "Mr. Finkelstein says your assignment is late!" and "I haven't seen you read a single page of Tom Sawyer!" and "This is unacceptable, Tobias!" and "Fresh starts" and all kinds of other stuff I tuned out because the point was clear.

And that point was: Toby, you'll spend the dying moments of your weekend doing homework.

Thanks a lot, Finkel-Fart.

Tuesday, January 15

TODAY MARKED THE TENTH consecutive lunch period of one Toby "El Machina" Solano sitting alone at a table for ten, eating burnt meatloaf and the occasional tater tot, washing it all down with about a gallon's-worth of chocolate milk if you add up all the tiny cartons scattered in front of me. Sorry. I had to throw in an "El Machina" there. I remember Dad told me, "If you want an identity to stick, you have to believe it yourself. You have to live by the name even when the mask is off." So I guess writing "El Machina" down in this journal a bunch of times is a good start. Although it's not like anyone will ever see this thing unless I pull a knucklehead move like Finkel-face and toss all these pages out on the streets of Mapleton. Like an idiot. And I am no idiot.

But I *am* still mad about the cafeteria

situation, because even though I'm no fan of Jimmy Baker, or Maya, or Derek Meeks, and I have no intention of ever being anything close to friends with a single one of them, it kind of sucks to sit alone. Like I have an infectious disease or something. Maybe they think uncontrollable, spiky hair is contagious. Who knows? All I can say is it'd be nice to eat my lunch and not stick out like a skyscraper in the desert for once.

And that's all I'm saying.

Except I'll also go ahead and mention the cafeteria abandonment issues I've been dealing with may or may not have fueled the incident I got myself into today. See, I was sitting there with my eyes trained down on my plate like you do when there's no one at your table but you and the soup du jour. If you ever had the misfortune of being in this situation, then you know how all your senses start working overtime. It's like being in the woods at night. Since you can't see too well, you hear things and smell things better.

Well, I heard all I needed to hear from about two table-lengths away, and I knew almost instantly it was Pitsniffer Baker. The thing that caught my attention as I bottomed out another milk carton was Jimmy's nasally whine and the words, "Toby...Solano...I think." But then Derek stepped in front of Jimmy and blocked his pathetic, little voice for a few seconds. Until I heard something come out of his pie hole that sounded like, "...and his size."

His SIZE?

Can you believe that?

I mean, I didn't hear what he said before or after these words, but does it matter? He could have said, "and his size...is like a walrus," or "and his size...would prevent him from sitting in a domed stadium," or "his breath is hot trash...AND HIS SIZE...is infinity." Who knows? He could have said all three. At the same time!

All I can say (and this is probably not the last thing I'll say, because who am I kidding?) is I made a decision at that moment. Right then and there. I wasn't about to let a no-good Pitsniffer like Jimmy Baker push me around. And when I make decisions, they're set in stone.

I waited for Jimmy to race to the food line for a second helping, because I knew he'd be the type of guy clueless enough to leave his milk behind for all the world to meddle with. Then I took a quick loop around the condiment station, selecting the biggest and fullest bottle of Red Hot Mama Lucia's Red Hot Sauce. And I casually twisted off the safety cap meant to provide a slow and non-excruciating drip-drip of hot sauce to your food, replacing it with nothing at all.

The bottle had been successfully converted to 'intense pour mode' and all I'd have to do was apply a volcanic dose to Jimmy's unsuspecting milk carton--which I did in one quick dump as I swept past his table and sat back in front of my tray to enjoy the show. I figured Jimmy wouldn't know what hit him until he was in the bathroom hacking up pepper seeds. I thought I'd finally get a few laughs out of Mapleton after struggling through so many boring nights in this dopey town.

I was wrong.

When Jimmy sat down in front of his carton, I noticed he wasn't in front of his carton at all-- or at least not the carton I thought was his carton. I had miscalculated by one seat, and the unlucky winner of the volcanic milk lottery was Maya Providence, totally unsuspecting as she nudged her glasses up the bridge of her nose and pushed the carton to her lips.

I tried to pop up from my chair, but my legs got pinned under the tabletop. I tried to shout her name, but the words dried up in my throat. It was too late. Maya drank it. All of it. In two big gulps.

It took a few seconds for the heat to register on Maya's face, but when it did, it rose in bright red hives and a million beads of sweat. Her eyes bugged out of their sockets like she was possessed by a demon. Her hair stood on end. She clasped both hands over her mouth and raced for the girls' bathroom in the far corner of the cafeteria. The entire middle school population crashed down on her in a tidal wave of laughter...minus one.

And that one was me.

Look, I didn't feel great about what I'd done. Maya didn't deserve to lose her tastebuds over a sip of old milk. I guess Jimmy didn't deserve it, either. Good thing nobody's ever going to read this journal because, if they did, they'd probably think I was a pretty big creep right now. Even I kind of thought I was a creep after it all went down.

That's why I confessed. I walked straight out of the cafeteria and right past my next class, and I didn't stop walking until I was on the other side of campus in front of Principal Rubrick's door. His assistant was out to lunch, so I knocked and heard a deep growl from the other side. "Come in!" And then I heard him grumble something under his breath like, "Cause these people don't seem to think I have a right to eat lunch."

I had to remind Principal Rubrick I'm the new kid and my mom, Cait Solano, is a new teacher at his school. He stared at me for awhile—much too long to give me any confidence he remembered me--and then he motioned me to have a seat in front of his desk.

"What can I do for you, Toby?" he asked with this great grandfather of a smile on his face.

The smile disappeared about two sentences into my confession. I told him everything. About my plan for Jimmy Baker and how it backfired. About Maya. About my soul-eating guilt. I left it all on the table or, I guess, on his desk because Rubrick had no tables in his office, which was weird but beside the point. The point is, the first thing Rubrick did was hit the intercom button on Room 416--that's my mom's class--and he told her to report to his office at once. At ONCE, he said--which I thought was a bit harsh considering it was Toby and not Cait Solano who was in trouble.

All I can say (see? I've said it again) is Mom took one look at me sitting in the principal's office and I think her mind raced back to everything that happened in El Paso. I could see it on her face. A look that said, "Not again." The look got worse once Rubrick recounted my confession to her, stopping every once in awhile so I could nod my agreement to all the horrid things he said about me like, "Here at Mapleton we view that type of behavior as irresponsible. Understand, Mr. Solano?" Nod. And things like, "We must provide each of our students with a safe environment. Understand, Mr. Solano?" Nod. And the worst, "We can't allow ourselves to slide back into old patterns. This isn't Texas. Understand, Mr. Solano?" Nod. But I didn't want to.

The worst part of it all was sitting there watching Mom melt lower and lower in the chair with each word that volleyed from Rubrick's mouth and seeing her eyes. How the tears were so close to the edges it seemed they'd flood her cheeks any second. But she held them back. At least until we got to the car, after Rubrick punished me with what he called "a heartfelt apology letter to Miss Providence," which I gladly accepted for two reasons. One:

let's face it, I deserved worse and Two: Maya deserved more than an apology letter after what I'd done to her. Even if it was an accident.

So, I'll start with the letter and it'll be the best apology letter I've ever written (also the only one I've ever written), and maybe that will be the first step in becoming a better version of Toby Solano. Maybe it'll be what puts the "El Machina" in my name. Or maybe it'll just help Mom see it's not me who has the problem. It's Mapleton.

Friday, January 18

THIS MORNING, I FINISHED the all-important apology letter. The one that would seal my fate as either the most heinous being in the universe, or as the new kid in town who happened to make a (hopefully) forgivable mistake. In case you're wondering, I was going for the second option when I wrote the letter. As cool as it might sound to be the intergalactic villain of the century, I don't know how far that route would take me in a place like Mapleton Middle School. Or in any middle school. Plus, I'd kind of rather have Maya see me as the new kid. As Toby Solano instead of as some brain-eating reptilian from a distant galaxy. I don't know why. It's weird.

So, I wrote something like:

Dear Maya,

You probably don't know me (because who does at this school?), but I'm the idiot who dumped hot sauce in your milk. I didn't mean to do it. Well, I meant to do it, but the hives and all the related sweating were supposed to be for Jimmy Baker. Not you.

I know that's not an excuse for how I humiliated you in front of the entire middle school, and I know we'll probably never talk again beyond this letter, but I wanted to tell you that if you ever did get to know me, then you'd find out I'm not really the world's biggest creep. I can even be nice sometimes. But not when I'm wrestling.

I hope you can forgive me, Maya.

Sincerely,
Toby Solano

I left the "El Machina" part out because I wasn't sure if a school-sanctioned apology letter was the right *El Machina* venue, even if it did provide an opportunity to further cement my future wrestling identity. I folded up the letter, stuffed it in an envelope, and carried it around in my back pocket all day at school. Every time I saw Maya and thought I'd have the guts to hand her the letter, my stomach would feel all weird and jittery, and I'd either walk right past her or stay glued to my chair. I decided the best (see: easiest and least heroic) thing to do was to stick around after the final bell and slide the envelope through the vent in her locker door when everyone cleared the halls.

I prepped myself for the special ops mission with a few shoulder shrugs and some light squat thrusts. Just to get myself loose. Then I turned full secret agent, ducking from classroom to classroom to avoid detection, bounding over all the empty waste bins and stray textbooks that lay in my path, until...well, until I realized this wasn't a special ops mission at all. It wasn't even a mission. It was nothing. This place was a ghost town once the clock struck three. The only soul on the hallway was Phil the custodian, and he didn't care what I did as long as it didn't involve unloading buckets of manure into all the classrooms.

So all I did was walk up to locker two-forty-seven and slide the envelope through the vent, where it'd be concealed safely inside until Monday morning. Crisis averted.

Plus, on the way out I slipped on a stray sheet of paper (I guess you could say I stumbled upon it. Ha! That's corny), which doesn't sound like a big deal, but when I flipped it over, I realized it was fate. The paper was a wrestling flyer, and the advertised match was tonight at Mapleton Auditorium. And get this? It was a title match. And guess who was defending his title for the first time since he'd won it? That's right, the Mort-tician. He was set to fight some wimpy-sounding challenger named Big Baby.

I wanted in.

The only problem was Mom grounded me for the entire weekend after the Red Hot Mama incident. All I can say is thank god for a first-floor bedroom and my sudden life as a recluse. Combined, all I had to do was finish my dinner with Mom and then burrow away in my bedroom--like usual. Mom didn't suspect a thing. And why would she? I've spent every weekend since we moved here holed up playing *Quadrant* (or reading secret journals).

I took my birthday money and crawled out my window around eight thirty, when Mom was in the thick of watching her music star competition shows. I brought a few other items with me in case any of my snooping classmates planned to attend the match of their lord and saviour--I assumed they would. I snagged the items from the bag of old Halloween costumes Mom stored in my closet. A blond wig, a red bandana, and a stick-on handlebar mustache from the year I dressed up as Hulk Hogan and everyone in El Paso kept saying, "Ohhhhh

YEAHHHH!" to me when they answered their doors, which annoyed me because that's what Randy "Macho Man" Savage used to say and he definitely wasn't Hulk Hogan.

But that didn't matter tonight. All that mattered was me in my seat in the back row of Mapleton Auditorium dressed like the former heavyweight champion of the world with five minutes to spare before Finkel-fart's big match. I used the spare time to scan the audience; to find the geeky Mort-tician fan club--my classmates--all dressed in their dorky suits and waving their handmade signs around like idiots. I could tell none of them knew the first thing about watching a wrestling match because, if they did, they'd save their energy (and their voices) for the real action, or at least until their favorite wrestler made his way down to the ring. Part of me wanted to jog down the concourse steps with my handlebar stash twitching in the wind and plant a Hulkamania-style leg drop on their entire section. Just to save them the embarrassment. But I let them have their fun.

I'm glad I did, because it was short-lived.

The match ended about twenty seconds after the bell sounded, when a clearly out of shape and somewhat out of sorts Mort-tician tripped over the referee's shoe and planted himself face-first into the canvas. From there, the signs waved a little less frequently and the chants from El Stinko's cheering section grew more and more quiet.

And who could blame them? Who wants to be a fan cheering for the guy getting dragged across the mat by a giant baby? I'm not joking, either. The Mort-tician's opponent? Big Baby? Well, he wasn't trying to be subtle with the name. His manager literally pushed him down to the ring in a stroller the size of an aircraft carrier. He jumped over the ropes wearing a diaper that would leave a shadow over the state of Texas, and a pacifier as big as a basketball hung from a cord around his neck.

After two straight minutes of being dragged around the mat on his face, it was clear to any wrestling fan with a clue that the Mort-tician was out of gas. Or maybe he had none in the tank to begin with. Whatever the reason, Big Baby kept hitting the champion with blow after blow. A flying clothesline across the Mort-tician's chest. Then a chest splash from the top rope. A devastating power slam, followed by a few vicious kicks, chops, and jabs as the Mort-tician lay defenseless in the center of the ring. Each form of punishment shrunk the fan club down a few inches in their seats, until Big Baby saw his time had come. His opponent was toast.

He climbed up to the top rope and hoisted the giant pacifier over his head. He stared into the crowd and said, "WAAAAAAAAA! WAAAAAAA! WAAAAAAAA!" This was really starting to get ridiculous. So ridiculous, I even felt sorry for Mr. Finkelstein, laying there all groggy in the center of the ring, just seconds from losing his belt to an oversized, pacifier-wielding baby. It doesn't get much worse than that.

But once Big Baby went airborne and brought the baby blue pacifier weapon down on the Mort-tician's back, and then flipped the champion over for an easy pin, I knew the laws of the wrestling gods had ruled supreme. As always. Only the worthy survive in the square circle. My Dad told me that when I was three years old, and it's still true today. I suspect it will be true two million years from now.

You know? Being seen in public as a Hulk Hogan look-a-like when it's nowhere close to Halloween was almost worth it to watch my classmates learn that lesson for the first time, and to see the looks on their unmasked faces when their hero vanished into the locker room and his belt was awarded to a whiny, little baby.

Tuesday, January 22

I SHOULD PROBABLY BE outside setting off an arsenal of fireworks instead of in my room writing in this pointless journal, because something amazing happened today. You ready for it? I mean, you might want to sit down before I write the next sentence because I'm about to tell you something truly unbelievable. You sitting? Good. Because today at school...someone joined me for lunch. Like, a real human being with a functioning brain and everything! Believe me, I was just as surprised as you are right now.

You want to know what was even more surprising? Well, that real human being—the one with nerves of steel and enough courage in her pinkie finger to take down Napoleon's army—was Maya Providence. The same Maya Providence I nearly melted into oblivion with a half a bottle of Red Hot Mama Lucia's.

I was two or three bites into my grilled cheese sandwich when she sat down, totally out of the blue, and I nearly choked to death because if there was one person on the face of the Earth I thought would never want to stand within twenty feet of me, it was Maya. So, I kind of just stared at her with a bunch of gooey cheese strands sliding down my chin. Not a good look.

Instead of launching out of her chair like a missile and exploding right between my eyes (which was what I deserved), Maya smiled and handed me a napkin. Then she pulled a wrinkled envelope out of her pocket and placed it in front of her on the table. I recognized it because it was the same envelope I'd slid through the vent in her locker on Friday afternoon.

Before I could move a muscle, Maya flipped her glasses up on top of her head and took control of our surprise meeting.

"First of all," she said without introducing herself, "I forgive you. I agree it was a rotten thing to do to anyone, but if there's one person at this school who understands how Jimmy Baker can grate at you like, well, a giant cheese grater slowly reducing you to shredded mozzarella, it's me. That doesn't mean you're not an idiot. Just that you're an idiot I happen to forgive."

I opened my mouth to say something, anything, but Maya held an index finger in front of my face and kept rolling. "I know what it's like to be the new kid at school. That was me a few months ago, and I wasn't exactly Miss Popularity. But there's no excuse for taking your frustrations out on other people...especially innocent bystanders who happen to wear glasses and just want to eat a few greasy tots at lunch and drink their milk without sacrificing their sense of taste to the fire gods."

"Sorry," I squeaked out in something much wimpier than a whisper.

"You already said that," she said, lifting the envelope off the table to remind me. "It's the only reason I'm sitting here. Because everyone in the cafeteria and probably in the whole universe does moronic stuff sometimes, but only a handful of them have the guts to own up to them in writing. I respect that, Toby Solano."

I didn't know what to say. I mean, it's not like I could thank her or anything. Not after setting a small forest fire inside her mouth. All I could think to say was, "It was nice of you to sit with me, unlike the rest of your classmates." Dumb.

She smiled at first. One of those sly smiles that says, "I hear you, friend." But then the smile vanished, and she flipped the glasses back down over the bridge of her nose and she was back to business.

"To be fair," she told me, "I didn't think you were interested in having any company at your lunch table. I didn't think you were looking to make friends with any of us. I'm sure my classmates felt the same."

"What would make any of you think I'd want to be alone? I mean--"

"Maybe when you trudge around school all day like a zombie, people start to treat you like one. I can't answer that question for you, Toby. All I can tell you is your classmates aren't the villains you make them out to be. Not once you get to know them, at least. Trust me on this."

"Why should I trust you?" I asked. "I don't even know you."

"Because you like wrestling."

"What does that have to do with anything? And how do you know?"

"Because you wrote it in the letter, stupid." She unfolded the letter and traced her hand under the line I wrote that professed my love for the greatest sport in history. "And it matters," she continued, "because I do, too. At least since I moved to Mapleton."

"You're not making sense," I told her. "It makes perfect sense," she said. "We have something in common, other than our mutual distaste for Jimmy Baker...and that murder attempt you almost completed on me last week."

"Again, sorry about that."

"I know. You told me. Remember?" I

nodded with my eyes trained on the letter. "Look, it gives us something to talk about. Maybe even something to help us build some kind of friendship. And with friendship comes trust, so you better start trusting me, or you'll have a lot of lonely lunch periods between now and June."

"Okay," I said. "I trust you. Happy? Now let's talk."

For the first time since Maya sat down she looked confused, like suddenly I'd turned the mental tides on her. "Talk? Isn't that what we're doing?"

"Not about our classmates," I said, "or about the hot sauce incident. Let's talk. Like friends do."

"And what should friends talk about?"

"You said it yourself. Wrestling."

This remark brought another smirk to the corners of Maya's mouth, and the glasses were flipped back up on top of her head in an instant. "We can do that," she said. Her eyes shot down to the surface of the lunch table as if some kind of magical wrestling topic would appear there and help her get this inaugural friendship meeting underway. Then her eyes flashed back to me and she said, "Okay, I've got something. The Mort-tician. I think it's sad for the MWF that he lost his title this weekend."

I laughed. And not like a normal, happy-go-lucky, you're-super-funny kind of laugh. This was the kind of dirty, snickering laugh you'd expect to come out of the lungs of an evil mastermind who'd just taken over the world. I didn't mean to do it. It sort of happened naturally when Maya seemed so heartbroken over the title loss of one of the crappiest wrestlers I've ever seen in action. "The Mort-tician?" I asked. "If you want my opinion, I think the MWF is better off without a wimpy loser like him hogging all the glory."

"Well, then I'm sorry I asked for your opinion," Maya said with her glasses suddenly clamped down hard on her nose. I felt the need to explain myself.

"Look. Wrestling isn't for the meek," I told

her. "You can't expect to lie around all day eating cheese snacks and playing with your cat, and then show up to fight in a title bout. All unprepared. I mean, these guys are professionals, or at least semi-professionals. If you don't come to the ring prepared, you might as well not come at all. Even a toothless, diaper dandy like Big Baby knows that."

"Is that so?" she asked.

"Yes. The wrestling gods commanded it atop Mt. Luchador and willed it so. Plus, my dad told me that one time and he used to be a big-time wrestler, so I'm pretty sure it's true."

"So you're saying the sport of wrestling is ruled by a bunch of ancient and unwritten rules that nobody's ever seen or heard, and if you don't adhere to them you're a total loser?"

"Basically, yes. That's what I'm saying."

"Do you hear yourself? Because you're approaching a whole new realm of ridiculousness."

"There's nothing ridiculous about tradition," I told her.

"There's plenty ridiculous about tradition," she shot back even before I'd completed my sentence. "First of all, traditions rely on everyone in the world having the same exact backgrounds, the same desires, and the same problems."

"Yeah, so?"

"That's not realistic. And it's also not realistic to assume you know why the Mort-tician didn't put in his best performance this past weekend. You don't know if he got sick right before the match, or if he received a startling phone call in the locker room before he approached the ring, or if he'd just found out his brain had been taken over by an evil warlock in the third row. You don't know any of that, so what gives you the right to pass judgement?"

"I'm a wrestling fan," I told her. "That's what we do."

"Well, maybe you should talk some sense into those wrestling gods of yours, because it's a pretty crappy way to go through life."

"So what do you propose I do? Join the Morttician fan club?"

"No," she said. "You should start by remembering today is January 22."

"Yeah? So what?"

"Well, why'd you think school was closed yesterday. It was Martin Luther King, Jr. Day," she said. "And I think you could probably learn a thing or two from him, because even if you don't want to believe it, his words apply to wrestling too."

"And what words would those be?" I asked, allowing a sly smirk to wash across my lips.

"Just remember this," she said. "Everyone wrestles for their own reasons, and the Morttician is no different. I happen to know how important wrestling is in his life, so when someone takes it away I can feel how devastating that must be for him. I can feel the pain of a tiny hole opening up in his heart because it's no longer filled with what he loves. You know what that's called, Toby?"

"What?"

"Empathy. I'm sure you've heard of it." I had heard of it--the act of standing up and walking in someone else's shoes so you can understand the world from that person's unique perspective. Problem was, up to this point in my life, I hadn't practiced it all that much. Still, it made me think of Dad. Of Carlos "El Carisma" Solano and his epic journey to the top of the Lucha Libre wrestling world.

It made me think about how much time and energy Dad dedicated to his craft, and how his time spent in the ring defined everything about him. And it made me remember how deflated and depressed he became in the days after his injury--moping around the house in his underwear all day, eating piles of stale potato chips off his own chest as he watched Mexican soap operas on TV, losing his patience with

Mom and me at the drop of a hat. It was sad. Even if I wasn't a fan of the Mort-tician, I wouldn't wish my father's experience on him in a million years.

So I decided to give Maya an honest answer to her empathy question. "Yes, I've heard of it," I told her. "But maybe I need some practice." Maya's smile told me she approved of the answer.

But she wasn't done with me. Not without one last nugget of wisdom. "You know?" she said. "Dr. King said, 'Life's most persistent and urgent question is: what are you doing for others?' Most times, I think that's a whole lot more important--and more realistic--than mindlessly sticking to the rules. Something for you to think about." She gave me a slight nod and stuffed my letter back in the pocket of her jeans before grabbing her tray and heading off.

I finished my grilled cheese and realized the most nutritious thing I'd eaten all day was Maya's food for thought.

Thursday, January 24

CONFIDENCE IS A FUNNY thing. I never thought about it much, but that was probably the most magical (and useful) lesson I learned during my "training" sessions with Dad at Valenti's Gym. Back in El Paso. Sure, he taught me how to wriggle out of an octopus hold before it turns into a dreaded, octopus cradle, and how to lift an opponent into a hanging full nelson called the "Cristo" until he submits, and a ton of other aerial moves that are too complicated (see: I'm too lazy) to explain.

But the best thing that ever happened to me at Valenti's Gym was when Dad's wrestling buddies laughed at me. Trust me, I didn't know I was learning a secret life lesson at the time. I was actually kind of devastated when I walked up to the speed bag for the first time, tapped it once, and then took the return volley square in the chin. It knocked me back a few steps, but it didn't hurt too badly. What hurt was the orchestra of laughter that tuned up about five seconds after I thought no one was watching.

In the cab of Dad's pickup on the ride home, he laughed and said, "That speed bag got a good shot on you, but we'll call it a draw." I didn't find it funny. In fact, his comment sparked a two-month streak of me refusing to punch the stupid thing again. I mean, what was the point? I wasn't trying to be Rocky Balboa or anything, and I also didn't want my wrestling identity to include wearing a big, red ball on my nose and size forty-seven shoes on my feet.

Then, one day, Dad came home from a match with one of those rainbow-colored punch balloons. The ones they attach to a rubberband that you put around your wrist, and then you punch the crap out of the balloon as it snaps back against your fist. He gave it to me, and I said, "Uhh...thanks," and then I left it on the floor of my bedroom for another few days. But then I got bored after dominating the *Quadrant* world for six straight hours, so I picked up the balloon. I punched it and it swung back. I punched it again, and it felt kind of good. By the time Mom called me in for dinner, I was slicing and dicing on that balloon like a rounder version of Apollo Creed. And Dad didn't try to stop me, even as I whistled the balloon past his ear as he tried to pluck kernels off his corn-on-the-cob.

The next time we went to Valenti's, I stepped right up to the speed bag before warmups--and this meeting didn't end in a draw like the last. This time, all of Dad's wrestling buddies cheered instead of laughed, and Dad gave them all this proud, smiling look that said, "He's my son!"

He sat me down on the apron of the ring after his workout and asked, "Do you know why that happened today? With the speed bag?"

"Because I practiced," I told him. "With the balloon."

He laughed. "No. What you did with the balloon was nothing, Toby. It wasn't practice. You didn't need practice in the first place."

"Then what *did* I need? I asked. "Because I think we can agree I definitely needed something."

"Confidence," he said. "You needed proof you had the ability to do what you needed to do before you could do it."

That was the moment I realized ability and practice can only take you so far. It's knowing how to believe in those abilities that adds the superhuman rocket fuel to the system. There's only one muscle that can do the job, and it's locked up inside your skull. It's your brain, stupid.

Of course, confidence can work against you if you're not careful. If you don't use it right. Like, if you've never been stung by a bee before and you start to believe you're invincible against the world's bee population, so you jam your whole head inside a hive without fear of your face looking like a piece of Silly Putty in your next yearbook picture. That's classic overconfidence because, trust me, you won't want a copy of that yearbook if you do the beehive thing.

Or you could lose every ounce of your confidence overnight and suddenly be a hundred times less able to perform a simple task than if you rolled out of bed and I asked you to rattle off the state capitals. You'd be out of rhythm. Unsure of yourself. Like I was after enduring that brutal speed bag beating.

Take my teacher, Mr. Finkelstein, for instance. I mean, I kind of thought he was a crappy teacher before he got humiliated by Big Baby and lost his belt, but now it's like watching the final, dying crawl of a zombie each time he mopes to the front of the classroom. It's sad, and the whole speed bag memory makes me have this weird feeling for the guy, like I can't enjoy watching his daily implosion. I sure hope it's not a super-contagious case of the empathy bug Maya told me was going around.

Whatever it is, it must not be too catchy because even Mr. Finkelstein's precious, little fan club members can't resist taking advantage of the guy in his nearly catatonic state. For starters, you have the snoozers. These are kids like Mandy Mallomar and Derek Meeks, who sensed the Fink was in no state of mind to be an actual teacher and pinned their faces to their desks for a full forty-five-minute session of sweet, midday slumber. I even caught Maya a few times this week with her glasses half-cocked and her face sliding drowsily down her palm before jump-starting herself back to life with the flicker of her eyelids.

Then you have the buffoons. Much, much worse than the snoozers. These were kids like Jimmy Baker, who saw Mr. Finkelstein's moment of weakness as an opportunity, because kids like the Pitsniffer can't resist trouble when trouble presents itself. So, here's a basic idea of what today's class looked like:

> *12:35 pm* - The bell rings and students file into Mr. Finkelstein's classroom. Finkelstein yawns, folds up his paper, and swirls half a cup of cold, stale coffee around in his mug.
>
> *12:36 pm* - The snoozers are in their

second dreams, and the slobber begins to puddle on their desks.

12:37 pm - Mr. Finkelstein limps to the front of the class and writes something on the board. It says, "Read quietly," as if he couldn't just mention that to us.

12:38 pm - Everyone (who's still awake) takes out a book to read.

12:39 pm - No one (but Maya and I) bothers to keep their book open anymore, as Mr. Finkelstein buries his face in the comics behind his desk.

12:40 pm-1:19 pm - All hell breaks loose. The Pitsniffer tears little scraps of paper off the edge of his notebook, mucks them up in his disgusting mouth, and then fires them through a straw (don't ask me why the kid always has a straw on him) at different members of the class--mostly the snoozers, who wake up long enough to gaze around the room in a daze before crashing again on their desks. And then, the whole thing escalates to a full-blown spitball war with Mr. Finkelstein shrinking back behind the pages of his newspaper as if he doesn't notice the battle raging around him. Then, the Pitsniffer organizes a full-class book conscious student in the classroom drops their heaviest books on the floor at precisely the same moment, to which Mr. Finkelstein simply grunts and ruffles the pages of his newspaper.

1:20 pm - The bell rings and we file past Mr. Finkelstein in silence.

I mean, the whole thing depressed me so much and I can't begin to understand why. Maybe it's because my mom's a teacher, so I know what would have happened to Mr. Finkelstein if Principal Rubrick had walked in on a scene like today's. Or maybe it's because the whole scene reminds me of Dad, and not one of the happy times with me and him at Valenti's. It reminds me of when Dad's confidence up and left him overnight. The night he destroyed both his knee and his wrestling career. By morning, he was almost an exact replica of what I see in Mr. Finkelstein's classroom these days.

I guess it wasn't just Dad, either. Mom and I also felt the draining effects of Dad's injury. The first few weeks--the ones right before he left for Mexico City (for "training purposes", even though we knew he didn't want to be around us anymore; didn't want us to see him as a failure)--it became clear Dad had already lost the charisma in "El Carisma". Like I said, he pretty much loafed around the house all day stacking empty soda cans and watching fake judge shows.

Mom went to work and came home with buckets of chicken or bags full of cheeseburgers, and went to sleep, and went to work again. Like a robot. They barely spoke to each other during those weeks. And I holed up in my room through most of it. Playing *Quadrant*, which is probably how my addiction began. When I stopped trying to reach out to people, because what was the point? Wouldn't they leave me for

Mexico City too? Wouldn't they get tired of being around me?

But I guess that's beside the point. The point is: I understand how Mr. Finkelstein feels. I know it sounds weird coming from me, and I still think the guy's a terrible wrestler, but Maya's right. He doesn't deserve to be treated like a terrible person.

Tuesday, January 29

TODAY I DROPPED BY Mom's classroom after lunch to let her know I'd be meeting some friends after school, and I didn't need a ride home. It was weird seeing her name—Ms. Solano—on the door placard for the first time, but once I stepped inside, I thought I'd been transported back to El Paso for a few seconds. Everything from Mom's old classroom was packed into the new one. The adjustable podium Dad bought her for Christmas one year stood at the head of the room, and the outdoor rugs with the Aztec designs I spotted for her at the garden center last summer were sprawled out under the window. The walls were covered in book posters that were meant to look like the billboard ads you'd see outside a movie theater while you're waiting in line. One for *The Hounds of Baskerville* with Sherlock Holmes peering directly at you through his magnifying glass. Another for Edgar Allen Poe's "The Raven", with a demonic-looking bird perched atop a human skull. And, of course, one for Mom's favorite play, *Romeo & Juliet*, with a couple of dudes in weird clothes swashbuckling on a cobblestone street.

I never read any of that stuff because Mom teaches eighth grade and I haven't gotten there yet. I tried to picture myself sitting in Mom's class, in this very classroom two years from now, but it made me want to cough up my lunch at the thought of still being trapped in this dungeon of a town so far into the future.

So, I shook myself back to the present--right back to my Mapleton reality--and rattled out my after-school plans to Mom as her next class rolled in.

Her eyes lit up like sparklers. "That's wonderful, Toby!" she said. "It's good to take a break from *Quadrant* and see the outside world." I agreed with her, so I didn't have to get into a whole conversation about how *Quadrant* is, like, ten times more important than anything outside. At least to me.

As soon as school was out, I did nothing at all resembling what I told Mom. I didn't hang around the schoolyard or meet a few classmates in town for a slice of pizza, or even go to the park to shoot hoops. Nope. I went straight down Dogwood Street to Zeke's Gym. Why did I go straight to Zeke's Gym? Because that's where the Mort-tician has been rumored to work out. And how did I stumble across such a rumor about my English teacher's secret whereabouts after school hours? Well, from Maya, of course.

All that happened was she sat down at my lunch table like she's done every day since last week and she said, "Please tell me why you look even less likable than usual today." I shrugged and nibbled on my ham and cheese sandwich. "I'm serious. You look like you lost your best friend while someone was simultaneously forcing you to smell the world's most heinous fart."

"That's weird," I told her. But then she

stared at me for, like, twenty straight seconds until I told her I might have some wrestling tips to share.

"What would I do with wrestling tips?" she asked.

I told her the tips I had weren't meant for her, and then her eyes got so big and super-magnetized behind her glasses I thought they might pop out and roll a strike across the lunch table with my empty milk cartons. "I see," she said calmly, even though every muscle in her body seemed to be twitching with excitement. "If you really want your so-called wrestling tips to be taken seriously, don't do it here at school."

"Where should I do it then? I mean, I'm already kind of leaning toward keeping my mouth shut and letting the Mort-tician fight his own battles."

"Meet him at Zeke's Gym. On Dogwood. He's there every day after school. With Sensei."

"Sensei?"

"You'll see," she told me. And she wasn't kidding.

For starters, Zeke's Gym was the biggest dump I'd ever seen. Cracked cinder blocks sputtered cement dust from the outside walls when the wind picked up, and there was a long strip of clear packing tape that appeared to be the only thing holding the glass inside the frame of the front door.

Inside wasn't any better. Not even close. The place stunk like if you smothered a pile of sweaty gym clothes under a five-layer dip of manure, pond scum, cottage cheese, foot cheese, and other assorted cheeses. Lots of cheese odor in that place, and maybe a hint of Wrench Body Spray mixed in there somewhere. To be frank, the place was a nasty, crumbling landfill with a few racks of ancient weights and some punching bags huddled around a flimsy-looking ring.

In other words, it was the perfect place to train a wrestler.

It didn't take long to spot the Mort-tician. After all, he'd be the largest mammal in the room, and I see him every day in English class. I didn't have to make much of a gamble in guessing the scrawny, wild-eyed madman dropping ten-pound kettlebells on my teacher's gut from the top rung of a ladder was this 'Sensei' guy Maya had told me about.

I found the darkest corner of Zeke's Gym, behind the heavy bags where someone (I assume Zeke) had set up a row of folding chairs for anyone brave enough (or lacking the sense of smell) to come and spectate. The first twenty minutes or so of the Mort-tician's workout was absolutely brutal. Some would call it pointless and stupid, but I'll be nice and stick to 'brutal'.

After Sensei air raided my teacher with kettlebell bombs to the midsection, I figured the workout was over, but then Sensei's nostrils flared wide and his neck crackled into a million tiny veins, and he started barking out orders at the top of his lungs. And, believe me, the top of this guy's lungs were so far out of the range of the typical lung.

"On your feet, Tubby!" he shouted at my teacher, which I thought was weird and also kind of relatable because that's what they called me in El Paso before I got tough. And Mr. Finkelstein scrambled to his feet, tapping his toes against the ground and doing all kinds of weird stretches I'll bet you'd never find if you researched everything ever written on the history of wrestling.

"Get your butt in the ring!" Sensei shouted, and Mr. Finkelstein scampered up on the apron and squeezed himself through the ropes. "Show me you're made of something!" Which I guess was Mr. Finkelstein's cue to go all Mort-tician mode on his random challenger, who happened to be a tall, skinny stringbean of a man with his hair tied back in a casual braid. He wore a short-sleeve polo shirt, some khaki shorts, and a pair of sensible shoes. If he weren't standing in the corner of a wrestling ring, I'd think he was a bank teller or a real estate agent or the neighborhood mail carrier.

Before Sensei even rang the bell, I could see the fear in my teacher's eyes. The uncertainty. I could tell he was standing in that ring as Norbert

M. Finkelstein instead of as the Mort-tician, and as soon as Sensei rang the bell, my suspicions were proven.

The Mort-tician never had a chance because Mr. Dad Jokes (that's what I call him) hit him with a spin kick to the gut and we all watched my teacher as he wheezed and coughed, and then fizzled down to the mat like a deflated party balloon--not much different than his performance in the classroom lately, I'll remind you. And that was the end of the challenge match. Mr. Dad Jokes stepped out of the ring, grabbed his cap off the wobbly rack, swung his official U.S. Postal Service mail bag over his shoulder, and I assume he finished his route.

I'm not kidding. The dude was literally a postal employee.

At that point, I felt the timing might not have been best for me to rattle off a bunch of wrestling tips. I decided to slink my way out of Zeke's Gym and reassess my strategies. But, before I could make it completely through the door, I heard, "Toby? That you?"

I thought about running, but then I remembered I'm not exactly a track star. It would be pretty lame to get caught spying on your teacher because he saw you high tailing it out of there at a casual jog, which is my absolute top speed. Don't judge.

I did the only thing I could do. I turned around to face the music, but there was no music at all. Not a single note. Just a maniacal, bald man and his mind-bending vocal cords laying siege to my eardrums. "Who sent you!? Are you a spy? How'd you find us!?" and all kinds of other high-pitched questions came flying at me from Sensei's mouth.

"He's fine, Sensei. He's with me." I recognized the calming voice of my English teacher and felt my heart begin to beat again. Sensei shrugged and walked off toward the water fountains. "Toby, what are you doing here?" Mr. Finkelstein asked when we were alone.

"I...uhh...I--"

"I mean, is everything alright?" he asked with

a look of genuine concern on his face. "Are you in trouble?"

"No," I said right away. "No trouble. I'm fine. It's just...well...I had this conversation with Maya a few days ago and--"

"Ahhh, Maya. I guess that explains how you found me here." I nodded slowly, not sure if I just got my foot in the door with Mr. Finkelstein or if I just got Maya in a world of trouble. "What can I do for you, Toby?" he asked, the look of shock transforming into a smile.

"Well...I was at your last match and--"

"It was a trainwreck?"

"Well, yeah, but that's not what I--"

"And I should retire from wrestling before I humiliate myself any further?"

"No, I--"

"Because I thought about it, and I came pretty close to hanging up the old wrestling boots."

"But you didn't. Because--"

"Because I'm here? Training?" His shoulders drooped and his eyes fell down to trace the cracks in the concrete floor. He looked about as sad and defeated as I've ever seen a person in that moment, but then a vibration rolled up through his chest and into his throat, and then it thundered past his lips in the form of a laugh. "Yeah, I guess I don't know why I keep showing up," he said. "I mean, Sensei would literally murder me if I'm not here at 3:15 sharp, but besides not having a death wish I don't know what keeps me coming to Zeke's."

"Maybe it's because you love it," I said, finally finding my voice enough to complete a full sentence.

"Toby, I'm not sure I love getting flattened by kettlebells every day."

"Not that," I said. "I mean wrestling. It's in your blood, Mr. F." It was the first time I ever called him Mr. F, like one of his lovestruck little minions at school, and it didn't feel too terrible. "It's like my dad," I continued. "He had to stop wrestling for awhile, and he became a different person."

"Like wrestling formed his identity and he

didn't know who he was without it?" Mr. Finkelstein asked.

"Exactly," I said.

He stared at me for a moment, and I could tell the cogs and gears in his mind were working overtime. Then he nodded and said, "You know wrestling better than you let on, Toby. I didn't know your father was a fan of the sport."

"More than a fan," I told him. "My dad was one of the best. He was Carlos "El Carisma" Solano."

"Your father is El Carisma?"

"Was," I said. "Before he got hurt." Mr. Finkelstein dropped to his knees and proceeded to bow down as if he were worshipping some kind of wrestling royalty or maybe even a god. Then he sprang back to his feet with a grin on his face. "Sorry about that," he said. "I get a bit crazy when I meet family members of my favorite wrestlers."

"Does this happen often?" I asked.

"First time," he said, and I had to laugh a little even though I fought hard to chew it back.

"Look," I said, "A part of me wants to sit back and watch you embarrass yourself over and over again, until the crappy MWF folds and I never have to hear about it again."

"Then why are you here?"

"Because Maya made me feel guilty. She used all kinds of mind control tactics on me, as far as I could tell, and she even pulled out famous quotes on me to rub it in."

"She fights dirty," Mr. Finkelstein said with a proud smile crossing his lips.

"So, I guess I came down here today to offer my services."

"Your services? And what do you plan to do for me, Toby? Call the ambulance the next time I get flattened?"

"If you listen to me, there's no chance of you getting flattened ever again. Your opponents won't be able to lay a hand on you."

He looked skeptical. Okay, so he looked more than skeptical. His mouth was dropped wide open so he could probably swallow a whole handful of flies, and the wrinkles on his brow grew so heavy and wrinkly I thought they might slide right off his face like hot cheese from an upturned pizza. "You do notice I'm not exactly the smallest target, don't you?"

"Doesn't matter," I said. "And I know from experience." I slapped my palm across my gut a few times to prove we faced the same challenges.

"I already have a trainer," he told me, and he pointed to the opposite end of Zeke's Gym where a scrawny man filled to the gills with rocket fuel was burning holes through my body with the flames in his eyes.

"He'd still be your trainer," I said with certainty, because I'd have to be pretty fond of excruciating pain to say the opposite with Sensei in the room. "All I'd do is show you some new moves. Teach you a new style. Get you up to speed with Lucha Libre culture. Just a few things to make you less predictable in the ring."

"Lucha Libre?" he asked. "You think I could do that kind of stuff? Like flying from the top rope and bouncing around the ring like a pinball?"

"It might take some time, but I think we could pull it off. And then we can set up a rematch with that Big Baby loser and get your belt back, and you can go back to moving through life as a human instead of a victim of the zombie apocalypse."

"Yeah," he said. "That'd be nice, but I don't think I'm anywhere near ready to face Big Baby again. Maybe not ever."

"Of course you're ready. It's only been two months since you beat the Theorem and he was at least four million times tougher than that diaper dude who beat you."

"How'd you know about the Theorem?" he asked.

My eyes flashed and my heart dropped down to my shoes because I realized I'd almost admitted to combing through the poor guy's journal. His private thoughts. The ones he warned potential snoops (that's me) against reading. But I recovered quickly, almost like if I got hit by a flying clothesline but needed to catch my breath and roll out of the ring to prevent further abuse. "Oh," I said. "Yeah, it's a pretty small town." This lame excuse seemed to satisfy the guy. Then the cogs started winding again in his brain and I knew I was getting somewhere.

"You know?" he asked. "I don't remember seeing your name anywhere on the sign up sheet for spring exhibition wrestling."

"That's because it's not on there," I said. He shot me a mock look of surprise that was so staged I think even Mr. Finkelstein knew he was being a fraud who'd been waiting for me to sign up for the team since the first day I dragged my massive body into his classroom. But I let him carry out the charade anyway because, well, it's wrestling.

"I'll make a deal with you," he told me.

"I'm listening."

"You sign up for the team and promise to stick it out for the entire season, and I'll let you come down here to Zeke's each day after practice and continue your training with me and

Sensei."

"And you'll set up the rematch with Big Baby?"

"One step at a time, Toby. First, let me try to get a hang of this Lucha Libre stuff you're talking about, then we'll see." I knew "we'll see" was the adult equivalent to a big "yeah, right," and the last thing I wanted to do was join a crappy, school wrestling team where I'd have to show people my skills and maybe (I'm talking the smallest speck of a chance) even fail.

"I... uhhh... I don't know," I said.

"Come on, Toby. It's only fair. You're not scared are you? Because if I have to jump in the ring with someone other than my actual mailman, then the least you could--"

"I'm not scared," I said with stone cold seriousness. "Of anything. Or, at least, not wimps like Jimmy Baker or Derek Meeks." I held out my hand and Mr. Finkelstein smiled so broadly I thought he'd swallow his own face. Then we shook on the deal. First training session is next weekend, and I can't wait to teach my new student a finishing move that's at least fifty times cooler and more lethal than the wimpy Final Nap.

Man, confidence really is a screwy thing.

Friday, February 1

AS I SEE IT, there are two kinds of dodgeball players. Those who drool at the very thought of exploding one of their classmates' skulls with the blunt force of a common piece of foam rubber, and the others (that's my team). Those with bulky glasses that fog up after ten seconds in a humid gym and prevent the crystal-clear vision it would require to actually dodge a whizzing dodgeball. And, of course, those (like me) with a slightly stronger gravitational pull-- which is a nice way of saying "super-slow, big dude is an obvious target."

I mention this because half the class (let's call them the Dodgeball Droolers) cheered (it was your basic standing ovation) when Coach Seam announced we'd be playing the world's most pointless sport in Phys. Ed. today. The other half of the class--which included me and Maya (let's call us the Dodgeball Dropouts)--sank lower on the bleachers and awaited impending doom.

Coach Seam apparently selected teams based on nothing relative to basic humanity, because every screaming maniac in my class with a rocket launcher for an arm or the ability to slip into Fort Knox without detection ended up on the Droolers side of the court. The rest of us Dropouts--those of us who excelled in other areas of physical performance that didn't include throwing, disappearing into thin air, or hunting down other humans with a foam rubber ball--huddled together on the same baseline, under the same basketball hoop that in no way protected us from the coming onslaught of Drooler firepower.

Coach Seam lined the dodgeballs up across center court like one does before a slaughter, and he blew his whistle--which meant it was on. For at least three full minutes, which is much longer than I thought it would take for Jimmy, Derek, Mandy, and the rest to pick each one of us Dropouts off like wooden ducks at a carnival.

I thought: that wasn't so bad. It could have been worse. But then Coach Seam went all Sensei Clement on us and lined the balls up across center court for another round. The cheers from one end of the gym floor drowned out the distinct moans from the other side. I'll let you figure that out for yourself.

Seam blew his whistle and we were in the thick of game two. This time, I got smart and hung back behind my teammates. I mean, I felt kind of bad for treating them like human shields, but then a dodgeball whizzed past and clocked Maya's glasses off her face, and I gained some respect for my strategy.

In the heat of the battle, with dodgeballs peppering every surface of the gym and my teammates dropping left and right like a sad scene from a Civil War battlefield, I adopted a secondary strategy to layer on top of the original one. I dropped to my belly and blended in among the fallen, crouching courageously behind Maya as she took four direct hits in my honor.

And then something weird happened. Reggie Sparks, the quietest kid in the class (and a pretty good tennis player if you want to know the truth), wound back and threw a dodgeball. He actually got a shot off for the Dropouts! And it was a hardcore sniper of a shot, too. First, it collided midair with another random ball whizzing in from the opposite direction, and then it veered wildly off course, plunking Jimmy Baker in the elbow and taking out Derek Meeks on the ricochet. A two for one deal! The Dropouts had life!

But not for long.

The four remaining Droolers, led by Mandy AKA "Lefty" Mallomar, circled in on Reggie armed with two dodgeballs apiece. On old Lefty's word, they unleashed their payload at once, and I watched in horror as all eight projectiles made glorious, simultaneous, and direct contact with Reggie's chest. He crumbled to the ground, leaving only a single Dropout in the field--one Toby "El Machina" Solano, a young man so skilled at the art of dodgeball that his patented strategy was to lay face down on the gym floor, cover his head, and pray for mercy.

At first, nothing happened. All was quiet. I thought maybe I'd fooled them with my dead possum technique. I thought maybe they didn't know I was still a contender in this pointless contest. But then a dodgeball one-hopped my face and I moved just in time to save my orthodontist about two hours of work. I was still alive...but did I want to be?

That question was answered in the next millisecond, as dodgeballs rained down on me like, well, rain. Somehow, through some kind of possible defect in the laws of physics, I managed to roll right and then back to the left and then right again--each time slipping between the raindrops without getting wet.

Behind me on the bleachers, my Dropout teammates came to life--maybe electrified by my beached-whale/ninja approach to dodgeball, and when I heard them cheering me on it kind of lit a fire inside me. It was almost fun ducking and rolling and spinning around on the floor like a breakdancer to avoid throw after throw from the Droolers sideline.

That's when I got a little overconfident. When I got tired of playing defense the whole time and decided I'd try to blend some offense into my game. There were stray dodgeballs lying all around me, so I basically had my choice as long as I could avoid the downpour blasting over me from the other side of the court.

I only had to crawl a few inches. Only had to rise up on my hands and knees for about three seconds. The dodgeball was so close I could feel it on my fingertips, but something caught my attention. Out of the corner of my eye.

Something floral.

Something red.

Something I recognized.

And in those brief flashes of a moment, about two million things happened at once. I grabbed the dodgeball I'd been reaching for and popped to my feet. I cocked my arm back and watched four corresponding arms on the other side of the court cock back into identical positions. All of them loaded with foam rubber artillery.

Then that red, floral pattern swooshed into view again.

Not directly ahead, but in my peripherals.

That's all it took to break my focus.

To take me off my game.

To take four, foam rubber cruise missiles to the chin while I stood there like a dope with a dodgeball still in hand, and while the chorus of boisterous laughter spilled down from the Droolers side of the bleachers. The kind of laughter filled with high-pitched squeals and words you don't want to hear. Words that stick with you like "chubby" and "moron" and "sad".

But that wasn't the most humiliating thing to happen to me.

No, that took place about two seconds after I nearly lost an earlobe to a wayward dodgeball. That's when I realized the random, floral pattern I recognized for some reason--the one that distracted me while I was under enemy fire?

Well, it wasn't random at all. It was on a dress. And that dress was on Ms. Cait Solano: Teacher, Grade 8. My mom. The one who walked right through our dodgeball game in her red, floral dress with a big smile on her face just to say, "Hi, Seannnnn!" to Coach Seam and watch his cheeks go all red in front of his (see: my) entire class. Oh, and presumably to make my life here in Mapleton even more miserable than it already is.

I mean, the only thing worse than the sound of laughter after I proved to be one of the least-talented dodgeball players of all time was the sound of every student (both Droolers and Dropouts included) breaking out into a long and mushy, "Ooooooooooh!" as Mom swooshed past Coach Seam and out of the gym in her floral dress.

Man, I hate this place.

Tuesday, February 5

I MAY HAVE TOLD Principal Rubrick I wanted to be a different kind of kid. A better version of Toby Solano. The kind of Toby who doesn't incinerate the tastebuds of the only classmate who knows he exists.

I may have made my newfound commitment to excellence known to Mom on the ride home that day, and I may have used the same little promise on Maya so she wouldn't think I'm one of the top-five worst people in history.

Well, I may have lied.

It's not like I meant to lie or anything. I mean, I wanted a better version of Toby Solano walking the Earth as much as everyone else. Maybe more. But sometimes you have to fall back on what you know. On the old bread and butter. The stuff that got you here, which I'm pretty sure I heard a TV announcer say when I was watching a Texas Rangers game with Dad, so it had to be true. Plus, I didn't have time to come up with a better option because I wasn't about to spend another day dodging whispers about Mom and Coach Seam in the hallways. In fact, my days of dodging anything (including foam rubber balls) were done.

And it's not like I was happy with Mom or anything. I mean, that nonsense in the gym on Friday with her stupid dress and that phony wave to Coach Seam? What *was* that? And what about Dad? It's like she was intentionally trying to progress my life from its current dumpster fire status to a raging, five-alarm landfill inferno, and I'm not happy about it. Not even a little bit.

But she's still my mom, and I knew I had to make a decision. Would I go full-scale, old-style Toby (the wicked prankster from El Paso) and defend her honor, or would I be a good little boy (see: a Mapleton wimp) and let my anger get in the way of my rightful duties as the future "El Machina"?

Today, I made that decision on my own.

Well, sort of.

It all went down in the cafeteria during lunch, where it seems most of my important life events are destined to occur. I walked in like I have every day since I started here at Mapleton Middle, but the similarities to my daily routine ended there. Instead of rushing to the front of the serving line in a desperate attempt to get the very first cheeseburger or slice of meatloaf off the line, I took the road less traveled.

To the drink station, where Mapleton Middle School's precious supply of watered-down lemonade lay unguarded. I reached into my pocket for the plastic baggy I'd concealed there this morning. It was rounded on both sides and filled to the brim with powdered laxatives. Sweet, sweet laxatives I'd picked up from Han's Pharmacy yesterday after school.

If you don't know what a laxative is, the best way to explain it is like if you packed six million bowls of chili into a pill or a powder. I mean, if you're looking to spend a few days staring at the inside of a bathroom, this is the way to do it. It was kind of weird being a kid in a pharmacy trying to buy a bottle of powdered laxatives.

Mr. Han looked at me kind of funny when I plopped my single item on the counter with a few bucks and some loose change. He said, "Retirement is treating you well, sir. You look good for your age."

I stared at him at first because I had no clue what he was talking about. Then I realized he was trying to be funny, pointing out my purchase was probably best left for an octogenarian. Then Mr. Han said, "You wouldn't be buying this to pull a nasty trick on someone, would you?" and I knew he was on to me.

I had to think fast, so I said, "Trick? Oh, no sir. I'd never use medication to harm someone. This is for my great-grandfather. He asked me to pick it up for him."

It didn't matter that I was exactly the type of kid who'd pull a nasty trick on someone, or that I planned to use laxatives to do it, or that my great-grandfather lived in Colorado and I'd never met him. All that mattered was Mr. Han suddenly saw me as the defining beacon of hope in my generation. He bowed to me and I bowed back, and then he told me, "Youngsters like you are the future," and he patted me on the back and gave me a free bag of chips, stopping just short of awarding me an actual medal for my service.

If he only could have seen me today in the cafeteria, standing beside the lemonade machine with a fat bag of laxatives in hand, the lid of the drink receptacle raised in the other, and a devilish grin knifing across my face. In that moment, I knew if I couldn't pinpoint the exact classmate who was instigating the rumors about my mom, then I'd punish them all with the sugary lure of their favorite drink and the future surprise of a few hundred trips to the lavatory.

But that's all it turned out to be. A moment. One in which my best judgement and my best self were nowhere to be found. It's a good thing someone was there to help me locate them.

"Can you pass the hot sauce?" she asked from below my perch atop the drink stand. The pouch full of laxatives was tipped against the rim of the drink receptacle when she said it, and every pair of eyes in that cafeteria was trained on a tray in the food line. Despite Maya's keen eye, my plot had achieved a ninja-like level of elusiveness. But Maya was the only one that mattered in this case, because you may have noticed she's basically able to talk a mosquito into going vegan.

"What do YOU want?" I groaned, laxatives

still hovering over the vat of lemonade.

"Well, let's see," she said calmly. "I want you to NOT be an idiot. That'd be a good start."

"We can't always get what we want," I snapped, and I raised the plastic bag over the preferred middle school drink supply.

"You're wasting your time," she said.

"I'm not wasting any *more* time," I told her, "listening to people insult my family members so--"

"No, stupid. I mean, if you dump the bag I'll just tell Mrs. Crumpet in the kitchen and all that will happen is you'll guarantee another meeting with Rubrick. Is it worth it, Toby?"

"You wouldn't do that," I said to her.

"There's a quick way to test me."

I tipped the plastic baggy back a few inches and stared through the lenses of Maya's glasses. She didn't move. Didn't blink. She was a real contender. Not someone to meddle with if you wanted to live a safe, comfortable life.

I zipped the bag full of laxatives, stuffed them back in my pocket, and climbed down off the stepladder beside the drink station. Maya stared blankly at me for a second. Then she pointed to the contents of her tray. "I got you a roast beef sandwich. With horseradish sauce because I know that's your thing."

"Thanks," I said. She nodded and I followed her to our regular table. She tossed the sandwich down in front of my usual chair and I tore off the plastic wrap and dug in. After all, I was pretty hungry even if I'd just attempted to poison half my school.

"How'd you know?" I asked Maya after we ate in silence for a few minutes.

"Easy," she said. "I didn't see you in the lunch line."

"So?"

"So? Come on, Toby. You not in the lunch line ahead of everyone else? I knew something was up. I didn't have to look far. I mean, you weren't exactly invisible over there hanging from the lemonade machine."

"No one else seemed to notice me," I said. "Maybe I shouldn't be surprised."

"Oh, stop feeling sorry for yourself!" It was the first time I ever heard Maya raise her voice-- maybe the first time she'd ever done it in her life--and I nearly fell backward off my chair. "I mean, why Toby? After what you did to me and I forgave you, why would you do it?"

I didn't know what to tell her at first. Part of me was still shocked to the bone that Maya had so much fire in her belly, but then I realized she deserved the truth. So I told her. About my time in El Paso and how people used to call me 'Tubby' instead of Toby, and how my life was just as miserable as it is now until I learned how to make people fear me instead of pick on me, and that all I'd been trying to do was go back to the old bread and butter.

She kind of scowled when I said that last bit, and then she asked, "So, your answer to the problem was to become the bully?"

I thought about it for a moment and the only truthful thing I could say was, "Yeah. I guess so."

"Is that what you want?" she asked. "To never know if someone cares about you or even has a shred of respect for you--I mean real respect--because they're terrified you might stuff them in a locker or send them to the nearest bathroom stall?"

"I didn't stuff the kid in the locker. I neatly hung him there. By his underpants." Maya's eyes reduced to narrow slits behind her lenses. "But no," I said quickly. "That's not what I want."

"Then stop being an idiot and start noticing you have a friend. Like, a real one who doesn't care if people call you 'butterball' or if you suck at dodgeball, or even if you use her as a human shield while sucking at dodgeball...okay, so maybe I do care a little about that last one."

"Sorry," I said.

But I was kind of glad I had Maya as a shield. Just not on the dodgeball court.

Saturday, February 9

I ALWAYS HEAR PEOPLE talk about "new beginnings" and how great it is to have them. Like, if you try out for the part of Peter Pan in the third-grade play and instead you get the role of 'stage crew' just because of what the music teacher described to me as "flight issues." I mean, I'm over it by now, but I still remember Mom telling me, "When one door closes, another opens," like it was some kind of gift I received to carry boxes around the stage in the dark. Or like in fourth grade, when I couldn't get the hang of long division and I threatened to boycott Mrs. Parabola's class altogether and Dad told me, "The easiest way to end something is to begin again," which I thought sounded cool at first, until I found out it was his clever way of telling me I'd spend the rest of the weekend practicing long division.

The point is, there's nothing easy about starting fresh, or being the new kid in town, or even trying to start a new routine. I'm doing all three and I dare someone to tell me to my face just how 'easy' my life has been since I wound up in this dump.

But today may have been a bit different-- maybe the first bright ray of sunlight I've seen in a forecast full of thunderstorms. Or maybe tornadoes. No. In a series of class-five hurricanes.

Believe me, the start of this brand-new routine (the one I started today) was anything but easy. More like excruciating with a side order of hellishness. That's how it is, I guess, when you show up at Zeke's Gym for your first agreed upon training session with the Mort-tician dressed in your sweatpants and your t-shirt with the infamous, silver mask of "El Santo" (only the greatest luchador of all time) printed on the front. And you're met in the doorway by a snarling, yapping madman with rage blasting from his eye sockets and bullets dripping from his pores, and he screams, "You're a crab now, son! A crab!" Right in your face! Sheer instinct (and a value for your own life) tells you to drop into crabwalk formation, and you scuttle across the cement on your heels and your palms until you crash face-first into your sixth-grade teacher.

"Good morning, Toby."

"Morning, Mr. F."

And those were the final and fateful words spoken between us over the next sixty minutes of pure and eternal torture at the hands of Sensei Clement.

First, he screamed at us as we climbed side-by-side on knotted ropes all the way up into the rafters of Zeke's Gym, where only the bats and the dust bunnies roamed. He screamed at us as he set a timer for five minutes and told us to suspend ourselves from the main beam while he bombed us with water balloons filled with ice water.

The timer buzzed and Sensei screamed at us to climb down the ropes, and he screamed at us to crabwalk ten more times around the perimeter of the ring, and he screamed some more as he counted our sips during a quick stop at the water fountain.

Then Sensei stopped screaming and handed each of us a blindfold. "Put these on," he grumbled. "Then get out of the way." I tried to look to Mr. F for an explanation, but all I saw was the inside of a blindfold. Then I took a balloon across the face and the ice water rushed down my shirt, and I knew it was time to dance if I didn't want to get hypothermia. I juked left and took a balloon to the thigh, drenching my sweatpants. I juked right and my chest was splattered in icy wetness. I jumped back at the same time Mr. Finkelstein jumped forward and we bounced off each other and rolled to the mat like a couple of water buffaloes in a pinball machine.

That's when the ice water balloons really started raining down on us, until the timer buzzed again and we flipped up our blindfolds to reveal Sensei Clement about two feet in front of us, his hands fully loaded with balloons. "More crabwalks!" he screamed, and the whole battery of rope hang torture, followed by crabwalk torture, followed by blinding torture went on in a never-ending loop that lasted another forty-seven minutes, but could have easily been forty-seven years for all I knew.

When it was over, Sensei bowed to Mr. Finkelstein and me, and we bowed back. Sensei said, "Good job." Just like that. Not like we'd narrowly survived the final hour of our lives or anything.

Sensei headed for the locker room and Mr. F and I crawled to the center of the canvas and plopped ourselves down in the middle of it like twin blobs of pudding. We were oozing out pain and soaked in our own exhaustion (and a little ice water). But for some reason, it felt kind of good. Like I had some kind of weird energy burning inside me even after Sensei tried his hardest to grind me down to nothing. Like I'd taken the first leg of an epic journey with no idea of what lies ahead, but I'm excited.

After a minute or two of just staring up into the rafters, Mr. Finkelstein groaned and said, "You know? I feel like a pickup truck slowly flattened my body, and then that pickup truck got flattened by a freightliner, which then got hit by a rushing locomotive, and then the whole mess got buried under an avalanche."

"I guess this is what it feels like to start fresh," I said.

"Yep," he said. "Could feel better. Could feel worse."

I nodded but, even after taking the full arsenal of Sensei's wrath, I felt a whole lot closer to the better than I was to the worse.

Monday, February 11

SOMETIMES I WISH THE world could be placed in a time machine and sent back to when King Arthur and his Knights of the Round Table enjoyed their reign. I mean, I know they never existed except in fairy tales, but there were real knights just like them in medieval times.

One thing they had was a code of chivalry, which was a set of rules to live by that all knights agreed upon even without having to write them down on paper. Or papyrus. Or whatever they used back then. Maybe it was called vellum. I don't know.

My point is, they enforced these rules on themselves and each other in order to create a world that made sense. That had more order than chaos. They were easy rules to follow, like "never lie" and "be generous to all" and "always fight against evil." But I guess the whole trick was doing the right thing when no one was watching. Come to think of it, I guess unwritten rules don't always work out well because, if they did, medieval times probably wouldn't have been such a dangerous place where people had to walk around wearing suits of armor.

It's kind of like in Lucha Libre, how there's an unwritten rule that says it's an utter disgrace to unmask a luchador and expose the wrestler's true identity. A *technico* (your typical luchador hero) would never do such a thing. But the *rudos*? The no-good, underhanded heels of the Lucha Libre world don't care about rules, either written or otherwise. They have no problem dishonoring a fellow luchador by tearing off the *mascara* after a defeat.

If you ask me, poor Mr. Finkelstein has a whole classroom full of *rudos* this year, because today they proved they followed no code of any kind, nor even an unwritten rule.

Today, Mr. Finkelstein was thirty seconds late for class because today (of all days) the poor man needed to use a toilet. And, somehow, those thirty seconds turned into a scene from the end of the world.

First, Derek Meeks stood on his desk and performed a medley of his favorite celebration dances from the game *Quadrant*, which I would have found interesting if Jimmy Baker didn't use the opportunity to plunk Derek right between the eyes with one of those oversized, pink erasers. That toppled the desk (and Derek), and then all hell broke loose. Mandy chased people around the room firing staples from Mr. Finkelstein's stapler, while Derek and Jimmy volleyed rolled-up balls of paper back and forth from opposite ends of the room. Even Reggie got into the mix, using his flexible ruler to slingshot wads of dried rubber cement against the board in gooey, brown splotches that looked like boogers.

But then one of those dried-up boogers ricocheted off the board and stuck fast in the middle of one of Maya's lenses and she lost her mind for the second time in a week. She popped out of her chair and shouted, "That's eee-

NOUGH!" so loud I'll bet Mr. Han heard her as he sold a bottle of aspirin down at the pharmacy. Everyone in the room stood still and fell silent. I mean, you'd think for a person who just snuffed out an entire classroom full of lit firecrackers by jumping from her chair and specifically shouting the words 'that's' and 'enough' with a pretty big exclamation point, that getting the room silent and in order would literally be enough.

But it was not.

Enough.

For Maya.

Nope. Good, old Maya always goes the extra mile.

She picked Jimmy's oversized, pink eraser off the floor and flung it haphazardly and angrily and in no particular direction. It just so happened that direction was out the door and into the unsuspecting cranium of one...well, THEE Principal Rubrick. Yes, that one.

He was in the room with flames bursting from his ears in an instant, followed by poor Mr. Finkelstein who'd just returned from his fateful toilet voyage. "Who is responsible for this?" Rubrick grumbled at us with every inch of his scalp the color of hot, liquid magma.

I looked at Maya and saw magnified tears well up under her glasses. And that's the precise moment I found my personal code of chivalry. That's when I truly got my fresh start. That's when I said, "It was me."

So, I have lunch detention on Thursday as my price to pay for being Maya's shield. I think it was a bargain. I'm also pretty sure she's, like, in my debt forever now. Or something.

Thursday, February 14 <3<3
Valentine's Day <3<3

I DON'T KNOW WHAT the big deal is about Valentine's Day. I mean, you have those disgusting candy hearts everyone tries to force down your throat, and they taste like if you dipped a piece of chalk in a big bucket full of chalk dust. And what about the poor trees? Think about how many we murder just to make those stupid cards with corny puns on them like, "Whale You Be Mine?" and "You Octopi My Thoughts." Then we dump them in the trash, like, two seconds after we detach the heart-shaped lollipop off the back of it. And don't get me started on the world's dopiest mascot. The Cupid dude? He's just some dweeb in a diaper who's basically a smaller, wimpier version of the guy who kicked the Mort-tician's butt.

You know, the new champion of the MWF (it's painful to write those words).

But the worst part about Valentine's Day is how there's some unwritten law (here we go again) that says every food item has to be part of a heart-shaped, pink-and-purple-frosted theme song or it's not fit for consumption. I mean, why would anyone want to eat a chicken nugget shaped like an internal organ, or a cookie the same color as an eggplant, or take a slice from a cake with a creepy-smiling diaper dandy perched on top? It's madness, I tell you.

Of course, it also kind of smelled delicious earlier today when I sat alone in Rubrick's office with my bagged lunch and served my detention. Banned from the annual Valentine's Day feast in the cafeteria. And all in the name of chivalry.

It was pretty bad sitting there, listening to the second hand on Rubrick's wall clock

TICK.

TICK...

TICK.......

TICK..............

TICK...............................

TICK, and eating PB &J with the crusts cut

off instead of festive chicken nuggets, and purple cookies, and baby-powder-infused cheesecake. But it got a little better (see: less excruciating) when a visitor popped in. I guess she knew Rubrick and his assistant took lunch at this time just like she had probably memorized the daily schedules of every student at Mapleton Middle, and maybe everyone else in Mapleton at large.

"So, this is where they ship the big, bad heroes," she said while I had a gob of peanut butter stuck to the roof of my mouth. She had a box in her hands, and it was heart-shaped and wrapped in frilly, pink paper with a bow on top.

"What's that?" I asked when I freed myself from suffocation by peanut butter.

"I got you something," she said. "My way of saying thanks."

"Why didn't you just say, 'Thanks, Toby.'"

"Just open it."

I pulled the bow and lifted the heart-shaped lid off the heart-shaped box and reached inside. All I found was a scratchy, brown section of cloth.

"What is it?" I asked.

"Unfold it, genius."

I proceeded to Step Two: Unfolding a

 Pointless Piece of Fabric. But when the whole thing was unfurled, I noticed it was not pointless at all. It was a *mascara*! A very worn-out and crappy one that I knew belonged to the Mort-tician.

"It's a knock-off," she said. "I thought maybe since you're training with him now, you might consider becoming a fan."

I slipped the mask over my head and peered at Maya through the scratchy cutouts made for my eyes. "It's amazing!" I told her. "And I don't even know what else to say."

"How about saying you'll go with us and sit in 'Mort-tician's Row' at his next match. You know...if that ever happens."

So, yeah. Now I definitely need to convince Mr. Finkelstein to set up that rematch. For the sake of the sport, of course. Totally not because

Maya would be there. With me. I mean, we can't have that oversized Cupid dude mucking up both Valentine's Day and the MWF. Can we?

Monday, February 18

IT SOUNDED LIKE A good plan when Mr. Finkelstein said, "Since we have off school on President's Day, why don't we squeeze in an extra training session?" When I woke up this morning with *Quadrant* on my mind, the plan didn't seem so brilliant. When I hit the front door of Zeke's Gym and a bony arm reached out, dragged me inside by my t-shirt, and jammed an eight-pound medicine ball in my gut, the plan transformed into an act of terror.

Mr. Finkelstein and I were on Sensei's time from that moment on. It was only ten o' clock in the morning, and there was enough electricity surging through the guy to make his arm hairs stand on end. And today's circuit was the most intense, the most unconventional, and arguably the most pointless training session I'd ever been a part of or even witnessed.

It started out with the medicine ball planted somewhere inside my rib cage, and then Sensei whipped a starter's pistol out from under the elastic band of his gym shorts and fired it at the rafters. "You're off! You worthless sacks of--" well, a whole lot of stuff I won't bother to write on these pages. Hearing the words was enough to send me running in a random, zig-zag pattern across the gym floor until Sensei popped up in my face and shouted, "That a-way, you buffoon!" politely redirecting me to Mr. Finkelstein on the other side of the ring. I handed him the medicine ball and Mr. Finkelstein sprinted his weighted-down lap around the ring, and so on and so forth for at least fifteen minutes, locked in an epic, winner-takes-all relay race with a team of medicine ball trackletes who didn't exist and probably never would.

When Sensei was somewhat satisfied with our relay performance (see: he was two breaths away from banning us from Zeke's Gym altogether--his words), he fired his starter pistol in the air like a Wild West gunman and shouted, "Gear up!" Then he kicked over a pair of empty water jugs that were just sitting there on the cement bothering no one. At first, Mr. F and I stood there confused, kind of staring at each other. Then we realized the water jugs *were* 'the gear'. Sensei wanted us to strap them over our heads and shoulders like insulated suits of armor. Good thing Zeke had opted for the stadium-sized water jugs. The big ones.

Next thing I knew, Sensei shouted something like, "Fight!" and Mr. Finkelstein and I instinctively charged each other like a couple of Gatorade-drinking rhinos, only stopping long enough to hear the sweet POP! of plastic on plastic. We bounced around Zeke's Gym like Sumo wrestlers inside a lunch thermos for longer than I can estimate. Until I began to think the inside of that musty water jug was my home and I'd never see the light of day again.

But then Sensei ripped the containers off our heads and shouted, "Next challenge! Leap frog!" This sounded pretty easy and also kind of childish, until Mr. Finkelstein stepped past the corner of the ring and Sensei launched a shopping cart full of bricks in his direction. All I could see were Mr. F's eyes pop wide open as the rattle of the caster wheels closed in on him and he failed to move a muscle. The cart mowed him down. The bricks spilled from the basket and the cart careened out of control and flipped. And the sound that drowned out all of this commotion was Sensei's laugh. I mean, I guess that's what you'd call it. More like the sound a cat makes when it coughs up a furball.

"Next up!" he shouted at me once Mr. Finkelstein was back on his feet and the bricks were reloaded in the cart. I stepped out past the ring and the caster wheels rattled forward. And then I had the weirdest thought. Like, why did Sensei say we'd be playing leapfrog? Then it hit me. Not the cart--though it didn't miss by much. No. I remembered a move Dad taught me back in El Paso. "La Pidola". It's your basic leapfrog move. And that's all I did. I waited for the cart full of bricks to barrel right up to me and I used my hands and split my legs to spring right over the top of it. Totally unscathed!

Now, the back wall of Zeke's Gym? The one that was directly behind me as I completed my death-defying transformation into full-on luchador? That's another story. 'Unscathed' is definitely not the word I'd use to describe its current state.

But the current state of my wrestling progress? That's looking good. Even Sensei said so. Well, kind of. He pretty much grunted three or four times and slapped me on the back, but I knew what he meant. And Mr. F? Well, he took a page out of my book (even though I'd taken the page out of Dad's book) and braved the approach of Sensei's dreaded shopping cart three or four more times, only getting totally buried again on one of those attempts and pulling off at least two picture-perfect *pidolitos*.

Sensei was so inspired by our performance today he decided to go easy on us for the last fifteen minutes of the session. "Freestyle time," he grumbled before disappearing into the locker room, which in the wrestling world (and probably every other world) meant do whatever you want.

Mr. Finkelstein and I decided we'd spend our last fifteen minutes in the actual ring, since we'd been training with Sensei for more than a week and had yet to set a boot print on the canvas. At first, we paced back and forth feeling awkward about gaining the power back in our training session. Then, Mr. F said, "It was cool how you pulled off that leapfrog move. I didn't know you were an acrobat."

"My dad taught me," I told him. "Talk about acrobats. He could pull off *tornillos*, *planchas*, even *hurricanas*. All off the top rope!"

"You think you could teach me a few of those moves?" he asked. "Just for fun. You know, to see what it's like to be a luchador."

"I don't think you're ready for aerial moves yet," I told him.

"Well, what do you think I'm ready for?"

"*Cuerda*," I said.

"What did you call me?"

"No, that's rope work. Building on your success with *la pidola*...that's 'leapfrog' by the way."

"Yeah, I got that."

"Building on that, I think I could show you how to pull off a pretty sweet *pidolarana*. It's not an official Lucha move or anything--me and my dad made it up--but it works. And it'll make you look like you know what you're doing out there."

"I like the sound of this *pidola*...what'd you call it?"

"*Rana*. It means 'pin'. It's an acrobatic finishing move that depends on how much skill you have bouncing off the ropes."

"But I already have a finishing move."

"The Final Nap? Snore."

"That bad, eh?"

"It's not terrible. I mean, it's effective if you're getting the snot kicked out of you and your best chance is to grab hold and not let go until your opponent's asleep. But it's kind of boring."

He looked at me like I was the first person to ever tell him the Final Nap was about as interesting as a summer camp for future stockbrokers. Then he took off running with no warning at all, bouncing from rope to rope and back again, crisscrossing the ring like a very large and very round heat-seeking missile until he finally reached his arms back and held himself fast to the ropes. I was kind of amazed, to tell you the truth. I mean, the Mort-tician looked nowhere close to as precise as this new version of himself. At least not in the match I saw him fight against Big Baby.

"You think I'm ready to *rana* or what, Toby?" he asked.

"Oh, you're ready," I said. Then I showed him how to catapult off the side ropes (which he clearly knew already), come barreling toward the opponent and, at the last second, slide down and through his legs like a ballplayer stealing second base.

"That's it?" he asked.

"No," I said. "That's only half of it. The boring half." That's when I showed the Morttician how to grab hold of his opponent's legs as he slid across the canvas, and then pull him back over his head into a cradled pin. "All in one motion," I told him. "Opponents never know what hit them until the ref counts to three."

We practiced the move a few times with me standing in as 'the opponent' and the Morttician bouncing wildly from rope to rope. Let's just say it's a work in progress, although he did manage to slide tackle me on the last try and it turned into something that loosely resembled a cradle pin, and somehow Sensei popped up out of nowhere (maybe he flattened himself down paper-thin and slipped under the canvas. Who knows?) and pounded out a quick three count and then shouted, "Get showers!" which basically meant the session was complete.

Afterward, Mr. Finkelstein and I sat on the apron of the ring catching our breath, and I figured it was the best chance I was going to get. So I asked him straight out, "Are you setting up a rematch with Big Baby or not?" I mean, I didn't want to be pushy or anything, but I also didn't feel like waiting until I was Rubrick's age for the chance to watch a wrestling match with Maya...and my classmates. You know, they'll be there too.

Mr. F laughed off the question like it didn't matter. He laughed! I mean, I have my crappy, knock-off Mort-tician *mascara* ready and waiting and the guy laughed. But I wasn't about to give up that easily. I was like, "I'm serious. It's time you get your flabby butt in the ring." Just like that, cold as ice. Or maybe it was more like,

"I really think you should reconsider, sir." We'll never know. All I know is I got cut off midstream when this lady I recognized from school walked into Zeke's Gym with a pair of terriers weaving around in front of her.

She walked right up to us with her two dogs,

who looked the miniature college professors of the doggy world, and she said, "Are we still on for lunch, Norbie?" and she tapped a spot on her wrist where a watch would normally go but where there was no watch as if Norbie (ha! ha! Had she just called him Norbie?) had lost track of time.

"Of course," Mr. F said to her. "You think I'd miss the Lincoln Tower of Pisa over at Dom's Bistro?"

"It's a giant pile of trash," the lady said to me in a loud whisper, with her hand not really covering her mouth so there was no chance Mr. Finkelstein wouldn't hear.

"It's not a pile of trash, Toby. It's a masterpiece. Piles of rigatoni and pepperoni and mozzarella and, well, pretty much everything else. Dom's does it every President's Day."

"And this is the first year I get to watch him eat it," the lady told me.

"This is Valerie," Mr. F said. "You might recognize her from school."

I told them I did, and Ms. Gluten introduced herself as the Mapleton Middle School librarian, and I assumed a close friend of my English teacher, the Mort-tician.

Then she said, "Really. I'm in no rush, Norbie. You two can finish your conversation," which was perfect because I wasn't done convincing Mr. Finkelstein that his rematch was more important to my social life than, well, just about anything else--except for maybe Dad.

But it didn't matter what I said to the guy, whether it was the sweet and low approach:

"Come on, Mr. F, you're a wonderful wrestler."

"You compared my finishing move to a financial convention."

Or when I went the logical route:

"If you don't fight Big Baby, you're wasting all that money on Sensei."

To which Mr. Finkelstein said nothing, but I promptly got pelted in the face with a water

balloon, presumably from the direction of the locker room.

Or even when I went into total burn mode:

"You lost to Big Baby! I mean, you lost to Big. Baby. Do you really want to be remembered as the guy who lost to Big Baby?"

"Give it up, Toby. I'm not ready for a rematch."

"Forget the RE-match. How about A match? Are you afraid of that—"

That's when Ms. Gluten cut in with the revelation that she somehow knows all of my personal business. "This wouldn't have anything to do with your new 'Mort-tician mask', would it?" She put heavy emphasis on the air quotes around 'Mort-tician mask' and my English teacher didn't miss it.

"You have a fan mask?" he asked me. "And why'd you say it so weird?" he asked Ms. Gluten a second later.

Ms. Gluten jumped in first. "Because Maya may have mentioned something about the two of you going to the next match together."

I jumped in next, to defend my honor. "All of us are supposed to go," I said. "Not just us two."

"Is this true, Toby?" Mr. Finkelstein asked, and he looked kind of amused like he was fighting back a smile. "You need me to wrestle so you can go out with...all of your classmates?" I didn't answer.

"Come on, Norbie," Ms. Gluten said. "It doesn't have to be a rematch. Toby said it himself. Any match will do." She winked at her precious, little Norbie and that was enough to set a whole chain of events in motion.

Mr. Finkelstein shouted for Sensei, who came sprinting from the locker room like he was escaping a fire, and then Mr. F told him to set up the fight. "For this Friday," he said. "Nothing too strenuous."

Then a weird thing happened to Sensei's face where his bottom lip and his upper lip formed into this 'U' shape that normal people call a smile but that I heard Sensei once refer to as 'weakness'. Then he sprinted off into Zeke's office to set up the match, leaving me to sit and wonder if I was the most brilliant young man on Earth, or the biggest idiot in the universe to have actually made this happen.

Before he left, Mr. Finkelstein slapped me on the shoulder and said, "One condition: you double down on the promise you made and show up for spring practice next week."

I nodded, because now I owe the dude big time.

Friday, February 22

MOST WRESTLERS HAVE A pre-match routine, a list of things they do without fail before a big match, often in the same order or wearing the same pair of underwear. Some like to eat a big meal or take a long nap. Others are more superstitious. They might hop up and down the stairs on one foot to scare away the evil wrestling spirits, or they may refuse to utter their opponent's name until after the match has ended.

Whatever bizarre tactic you could think of, I'll bet wrestlers somewhere on this planet have used it to perfect their own personal pre-match routines. So, why did I feel so weird about the routine I put myself through tonight before the Mort-tician's big match at Mapleton Auditorium? I mean, I don't usually spend twenty minutes in the shower, massaging avocado-infused conditioner into each tender follicle on my head. And you'll rarely catch me rifling through the shoe box under the sink that's filled with bottles of Dad's old aftershave, because guess what? I don't shave yet.

But there I was tonight before Mr. F's comeback match, standing in front of the mirror with my face ablaze in Old Spice and my hands working overtime to pluck each strand of my black hair until it stood straight up. Just so I could smash it under a ratty Mort-tician mask and watch a wrestling match in a sweaty auditorium with Maya...and the rest of my classmates.

Mom drove me to the match and agreed to give me some space and come back to pick me up afterward. "Don't forget to call me," she said as I stepped out of her car. "So I'll know when to get you." I told her I would, and thanked her, and then waited for her car to pull away before I turned to search for Maya.

She wasn't hard to spot, standing beside the front gate in her fuzzy, brown suit jacket with the sleeves cut off. No one else in the vicinity of Mapleton Auditorium looked even half as ridiculous, except maybe the Mort-tician himself.

"Did you bring it?" she asked the second I approached. I pulled the mascara out of my back pocket and slipped it over my head. "Perfect," she said.

We bought our tickets and stepped through the turnstile, and I followed Maya down to section J-9, which was apparently better known as 'Mort-tician's Row" to at least nine other people in a tiny, suburban town that nobody's ever heard of. You know, the rest of my classmates.

But when we got to our seats and looked around, it appeared 'the rest of our classmates' had either turned themselves invisible, been abducted in the middle of the night by space aliens, or simply decided not to come. I'll leave it up to you to decide which of these options sounds most logical.

The real problem wasn't that all of our

classmates stayed home because, let's face it, I wasn't about to lose sleep because I didn't get to see the Pitsniffer tonight. The real problem was the sea of empty seats around Mort-tician's Row, and at the direct center of it, two tiny islands--me and Maya.

We looked at each other and neither one of us said a word at first, but it was pretty obvious our brains were reeling with a million questions. Like, what do we say to each other? And, why in the world are my earlobes suddenly sweating? And, are we, like, on a date now? And so many others I'm pretty sure my head will detonate if I ever have to think about them again.

Then Maya made matters worse by trying to say something (see: anything) to break the silence. "I hear they may fix the plumbing in this place," she said.

"Yeah," I said. "I mean...yeah." Smooth, cowboy. I'd never been so glad to be partially hidden behind a dopey Mort-tician mask in my life. Thankfully, the ringside bell rang and the PA announcer stepped to the middle of the floor--specifically to save me from this agony. And, also, to start the match.

Turns out the Mort-tician was set to fight some lame-o nobody named Triple S, which Maya quickly informed me stood for 'Selfie Stick Saul', which I guess was the obvious reason he went by the former. He came barreling down the concourse to the ring dressed in a white, Armani suit jacket with matching, white shorts that had pleats in them, and the whole time he was busy snapping pictures of himself on his phone. Like, this dude literally loved the camera and I'm guessing the camera loved him back, which is more than a little weird to write.

So I'll stop.

The Mort-tician approached the ring next, and Maya and I sprang to life. We may have been the only two spectators in the whole auditorium standing on our chairs and screaming our heads off for Mr. Finkelstein, but at least we were back to talking again.

Sort of.

The bell rang and the two wrestlers circled

the ring, feeling each other out. Then Selfie Stick Saul launched himself off the mat and hit the Mort-tician with a devastating dropkick to the head, and things started looking a whole lot like the last match I'd watched. Saul drilled the Mort-tician with an elbow drop, then a leg drop, then a flying headbutt. For a few minutes, I couldn't figure out why this Triple S guy was such a scrub and not the champion of the MWF. He wasn't half bad.

But then I got my answer. The stupid idiot climbed up on the second rope with the Mort-tician still gasping for air on the mat. He faced the crowd...and he pulled out his phone. I couldn't believe my eyes, but he actually stood there taking pictures of himself until I guess he was satisfied with the mid-match photoshoot and he stepped down off the ropes...only to take the weight of a Mort-tician-sized clothesline square in the chest. Triple S flew backward and flipped over the top rope. He plummeted to the cement outside the ring, and that's when the Mort-tician opened up shop on him.

He slid under the bottom rope and peeled that selfie-obsessed dweeb off the floor. He ran him into the steel safety cage in front of the crowd. He picked him up again and smeared him across the outside of the ring a few more times before tossing poor, old Saul back under the bottom rope like a bag of potatoes.

If I didn't know better, I would have said Mr. Finkelstein was having himself a bit of fun, but I'm not sure he's legally allowed to have fun. I mean, he's my English teacher.

A few kicks and chops later, the Mort-tician captured Triple S in the Final Nap and you could see the energy slowly drain from the guy until he was almost out cold. But then the Mort-tician did the unthinkable. He released his grip, just enough to keep Triple S woozy and wobbling on his feet at center ring. That's when the Mort-tician launched himself off the side ropes, slid through Saul's teetering legs, and put him away with a perfectly executed pidolorana. One...two...three! That was it!

The auditorium erupted in bonkermania.

Maya jumped on my back and gave me a bear hug, and I shouted, "I taught him that move!" though I'm not sure anyone could hear me through the pandemonium.

The ref raised the Mort-tician's arm in victory and that's the exact moment I knew Sensei and I were back in the rematch business. It would just take a little time. And a few prayers.

Maya and I were in such good spirits, we decided to stick around for the main event, which pitted a no-name newcomer against Big Baby in his first title defense since embarrassing my English teacher. Of course, as a wrestling aficionado, I knew that first title defenses are usually set up against creampuff opponents in order to give the champion an opportunity to build on the legend. So, I was expecting to see another cry-athon, with Big Baby wailing alot and then whaling on this guy (who just called himself 'The Champ', which was odd) with his prehistoric-sized pacifier.

I was wrong.

I won't go into detail, but this Champ dude? Wow. He looked real tonight. First of all, he came out in a proper mascara--electric blue--and his back was covered in this tough-looking tattoo that read 'El Rey' or 'the king'. And man, he wasn't kidding. In less than two minutes, The Champ hit Big Baby with plancha after tornillo from all four corners of the top  rope. And if you don't know what those terms mean, think of it as a one-man dive-bombing mission that completely obliterated its target: Big Baby.

There was a new champ in town, and there wasn't much chance anyone would forget his name. But that wasn't what was on our minds when the Mort-tician came out of the locker room dressed as Mr. Finkelstein, and he and Ms. Gluten paid a visit to Mort-tician's Row.

"Did everyone leave before the main event?" Ms. Gluten asked Maya when she saw all the empty seats.

"Yeah," she said. "Except they left before the undercard."

"I see," Ms. Gluten said, and I'm still not sure what she thought she had seen, but Maya nodded so it must have been something.

"Why don't you and Toby join us for ice cream," Ms. Gluten asked. We agreed, and we hopped in Ms. Gluten's car and shuttled over to Jerry's Freeze Shack so fast I may have forgotten to call Mom and tell her the match was over. But then I saw great mounds of whipped cream piled up on rivers of chocolate sauce, and I figured she could probably wait until after I inhaled a quick banana split.

We took stools at the counter, since Jerry's was set up to look like one of those classic, 50s soda shops. Mr. Finkelstein ordered for everyone and then he was like, "My treat! For proving I still got it, and for having people in my life I'm lucky enough to call witnesses." I thought that was pretty cool, because the only thing better than a winning wrestler--as I see it-- is a free banana split.

I dug into the cookie dough goodness of it all, and that's when I finally started to feel comfortable. For the first time of the night if I'm really being honest. And when I'm eating banana splits and feeling comfortable, I like to talk. And when I talk, I talk wrestling, and sometimes I talk Toby.

So, I just came right out with it as Maya and Ms. Gluten and Mr. Finkelstein were up to their tonsils in ice cream. "I miss my dad," I said. They all stopped eating and stared at me without a clue of how to respond. Of how to make me feel better. But I wasn't looking to feel better. I was only looking to talk. To get a few things off my chest. So I continued. "He's so far away. I know he's training and it's important to him, but what if he can't make it back?"

"To El Paso?" Maya asked.

"No."

"To Mapleton?" asked Ms. Gluten.

"No. To wrestling. I mean, it's bad enough he had his career ripped away from him by an evil rudo named El Ciclon--the tornado--who had no respect for the luchador code."

"What'd he do?" Mr. Finkelstein asked.

"He fought dirty. Like, all the time. But the worst thing was, he was known to defeat his opponents using highly controversial moves."

"Like, illegal ones?" Maya asked.

"Some would say so," I told her. "My dad included. I mean, what else would you call it when a wrestler brings a folding table into the ring and then elbow drops his opponent directly through it."

"Sounds illegal," Mr. Finkelstein said.

"Whatever you want to call it, it's what got my dad. It's what ended El Carisma."

"That's terrible," Maya said. "Does this El Ciclon guy still wrestle?"

"I don't know," I said. "He disappeared after the match. There was talk he'd been banned from the sport, but I think that's all it was. Talk. The guy just vanished. Maybe he took on a new identity. It doesn't matter."

"You're right," Mr Finkelstein said. "He doesn't matter. All that matters is your dad. You don't name yourself El Carisma unless you have a whole lot of heart stored up inside you."

"If your dad is even half as resilient as you, Toby, he'll be back in the ring in no time," Ms. Gluten told me. I smiled. But the smile vanished as quickly as it appeared, and it had nothing to do with Ms. Gluten's compliment or Dad's injury or even El Ciclon. It had everything to do with the jingle of a bell above a door leading into a certain 50s-inspired ice cream shop.

It was Mom. The woman I'd painfully neglected to call. I imagined her cheeks would be all red and her hair all disheveled with the rage I'd probably helped build up inside her by this point. I braced myself for the fallout.

But then she slipped completely through the door and her hair was neatly combed and her cheeks were perfectly radiant, and she was laughing about something. Then someone else slipped through the door behind her and that someone was Coach Seam--and the only person with rage boiled up inside him at that moment was El Machina himself.

I popped up from the diner stool, leaving half my banana split uneaten (the horror!), and I stuttered something incoherent like, "I gotta game. Go to...bed," or maybe even something dumber. Who knows? I was mad.

All I know is I snuck out of that place so quickly and so elusively I dare any ninja out there to match me. Nobody saw me (and I mean nobody), nobody said anything to me, and nobody should ever ask me why I walked back home. In the dark. Alone.

Not even Maya.

Tuesday, February 26

I'VE KEPT MY HEAD down since Friday's ice cream parlor incident because I don't feel like explaining to Maya why I bolted without saying 'goodbye' or finishing my ice cream (which was really not like me). So, I brought my lunch from home the past two days and found a spot in the back of the music room, behind the racks of old theater costumes and the boiler, where I sat among the cobwebs and ate my peanut butter and jelly sandwich in peace, without Maya or Mr. Finkelstein or my mom or Coach Seam to ruin it for me.

Look, I know it's not the best strategy or anything, and all it gave me was more time to think about Mom, giggling with her stupid ice cream cone in hand, and how I stormed out into the night and walked around Mapleton for a while, and how I still got home before Mom.

And how she walked in the kitchen and

didn't say a word to me. She just opened the fridge and stared in at the food without taking a single thing. And she kept humming this corny tune that reminded me of something an old person like Mr. Finkelstein might listen to-- maybe something like REO Speedwagon.

Wow.

Then I said something to break the silence and to prevent me from putting my fist through the table. "Mr. Finkelstein gave Maya and me a lift home," I told her, which wasn't the truth but I didn't want to get into it with her, and I thought she'd genuinely want to know--being my mother.

But all she said was, "That's nice, honey," before she disappeared into her bedroom where I heard her whisper into her phone for at least another hour before I nodded off. She never asked me about the match. Or Maya. Or anything. Ever since Friday, she's been walking around in this weird, little daze from fairytale land, and it kind of makes me want to puke up a pixie. Or a pixie stick. Or something.

I mean, there's bound to be vomit one way or another. It could happen at an ice cream parlor, or it could happen like it did today at my first official practice of the spring wrestling season. I've only been to one practice, and I already hate every second that's ever existed in the history of fake wrestling (which is what I call it).

For starters, they expect you to squeeze into this weird tube with a bunch of octopus tentacles hanging off it and two holes for your legs. Mr. Finkelstein called it a 'singlet' when he handed it to me in the locker room, but I think it should at least be called a quadruplet because it took three of my teammates (and myself) working in total unison to get the straps over my shoulders before the whole thing slingshot off into outer space and covered the sun.

Then, there's the whole 'training' part of the sport, which has nothing to do with acrobatic jumps, flips, or dives and everything to do with running up and down stairs. That's it. See stair. Run up stair. See no more stair? Run down stair.

Repeat. Thirty minutes of that nonsense and we hadn't even left the locker room yet.

By the time we got to the mat, I felt like--well, I felt kind of like I'd been through one of Sensei's workouts only without all the screaming. I guess Coaches Finkelstein and Seam held their vocal cords in higher respects. When we finally broke free from the sweaty, locker room air and made our way to the ring, I noticed two things right away:

There were no ropes around this ring; in fact, there was no ring. Only a bunch of dry-rotted mats.

Mom was sitting in the stands with a few faculty members from her eighth-grade team.

It felt pretty good to know that after ignoring me all weekend and most of this week, she'd still remembered about my big, fake wrestling debut and had come out to support.

The good feeling didn't last long. Only about as long as it took Coach Seam to blow his big, stupid whistle and shout, "Baker! Solano! You're up!" I didn't know what that meant. I didn't know much of anything about this fake version of the sport, to be honest. I mean, no ropes to bounce off and no bell? There weren't even spare folding chairs lying around to create some extra pandemonium. Only me, Jimmy Baker, and our headgear. And about sixty extra pounds on my side of the scale. I mean, I was pretty sure I knew where this match was headed.

So I lunged at him, and Jimmy spun around behind me, gripped me around the waist, and cut me down to the mat like a pine tree. Then he had his arms under my leg and the back of my head, and his hands clamped tight in two seconds flat. A cradle hold! I screeched like Big Baby until Coach Finkelstein said, "That's enough, Baker!" and then I just laid there looking up at the ceiling for a few seconds, wondering how I'd been embarrassed by an eighty-pound pitsniffer in what appeared to be record time.

My first instinct was to look up in the stands to see if Mom had witnessed the disgrace. But she was looking down at her phone and typing a bunch of stuff into the screen at breakneck speed, so I figured I got lucky.

I did not.

Get lucky.

At all.

Because Coach Seam was apparently not satisfied with seeing me get tossed around the mat by an eighty-pound pitsniffer. He also wanted to see me get skewered by a seventy-pound sniffer of pits. "Meeks! You're next!" Seam shouted. "Solano...stay on!"

I'd barely reached my feet from the Baker splashdown when Derek Meeks charged me like a drenched ferret. And I just stood there in my best impression of a pile of dried leaves that Derek scooped up by the stems and tied up in one of those massive, black trash bags. In case you're wondering, the trash bag was me. I was also the leaves inside and everything else that lay pinned under that scrawny (and surprisingly strong) rodent. As I fought (and failed) to raise a shoulder off the mat and prevent a second, humiliating defeat in the span of two minutes, my eyes found their way to the stands. Back to Mom. With her face still trained on the screen of her phone, and her fingers typing a mile a minute. And she was giggling. Missing every disgraceful second of what had happened to her son on the mat. And I was thankful.

But only for a second.

Until I remembered. The giggle. The one I'd seen before with her eyebrows all scrunched up into her forehead and her smile at an odd angle on her face. At the ice cream parlor. With Seam.

Then it all happened at once. My eyes worked back and forth from Mom to Seam and back again, noting the pattern of read-giggle-type-send move in a wave from Mom's phone. To Seam's phone. Then back to Mom's phone. And Coach Finkelstein dropped to the mat on his belly to inspect the two centimeters of daylight between my shoulders and the mat. Then one centimeter. Then no centimeters.

Then it was over. All of it. Practice, my two worthless matches, and any desire I had to stick around and watch the text messages bounce back and forth off those gym walls like Cupid's heart-shaped farts.

Man, who knew wrestling could suck this bad?

Friday, March 1

SO, WRESTLING PRACTICE KIND of sucked on Tuesday, and I wasn't exactly in the mood to run into that giggling, text fool Coach Seam, so I decided one day of fake wrestling was more than enough for the week. I mean, Mr. Finkelstein can't expect me to hold up my end of our wrestling bargain *and* watch my own mom have her first middle school crush all over again right before my eyes, can he?

What I did was I treated the ends of the days this week like any other day. I got my books from my locker, walked toward the gym for wrestling practice, and then walked right past it onto Maple Avenue, where if you go a block or two, you'll run straight into Zippy's Convenience Store on the corner of Sweet Gum Drive.

Old Zippy (I assume he's the guy behind the

counter) has a few tables and chairs inside the establishment, and I spent the past few afternoons sitting at a patio table near the chip aisle, sipping on a cola-flavored slushie and eating package after package of powdered donuts. It was glorious. So much healthier than subjecting myself to another minute of fake wrestling, or cheesy love stories.

But today didn't go as planned. I sat down at my usual table and took a long, refreshing swig of my usual slushie. Got a brain freeze and everything, just like I always do.

That's when things got weird.

At first, I just kind of felt it. Like someone hovered over me, watching my every move. But the store was pretty empty, so I split the cellophane on my donuts and that's when I truly felt something. In my face. And it was a rancid track shoe connected to a spin-kicking wild man in midflight!

My donuts splattered against the drink case, crumbled down the glass doors, and came to a rest in a powdery pile on Zippy's spotless floor.

Sensei rose from a crouched position with his eyes ablaze and trained right on me.

"You're a crab!" he shouted, and I almost jumped down from the comfort of my patio furniture to obey the order before I realized I was eating donuts (or at least I was trying to) in Zippy's Convenience Store and not being reduced to dust in Zeke's Gym.

"No chance," I said.

Bad move.

Sensei barely flinched. All I saw were his teeth clench down a little harder and his leg kick out at the speed of light and make contact with the leg of the chair I was sitting on--and then I wasn't sitting on it anymore. No, in the flash of an eyelid, I was down on Zippy's tile floor in full crabwalk formation.

"You're a crab now; you giant strudel! WALK!" I wasn't about to make another false move because I was running out of props for Sensei to kick that weren't intended to be attached to my body forever.

So, I walked. Like a crab. Down the chip aisle

and out of Zippy's Convenience Store. Across the intersection at Maple and Sweet Gum, and all the way through Veteran's Park at the center of town until we reached the parking lot of Zeke's Gym.

I never knew until today, but Zeke's Gym has ample parking. Thirty-six individual parking spots, to be exact, not counting the two handicap spots in front of the door. I know this now because, once I completed my crabwalking tour of Mapleton, Sensei screamed, "On your feet, you sluggish cruller!" and then he had me tour each parking spot with twenty, bare-knuckle pushups--and, in case you're wondering, Sensei did count the handicap spots. Twice.

By the time we got inside the actual gym, I wished I'd just shown up at fake wrestling practice, where Coach Finkelstein probably would have been handing out powdered donuts with the headgear. But not here. Not with Sensei.

Not as things started to get real.

It started out with work on the speed bag, which is pretty normal unless you're practicing headbutts over and over again, pitter-pattering off your hollow gourd until you feel like you may never have a coherent thought again. Then a few more donut-related insults from Sensei like, "Knock those sprinkles right off the bag!" and "Would you hit it harder if it were jelly-filled?" and "You've got some donut holes in your head!" which I personally didn't find to be his best work, but I wasn't about to tell him so.

After a few more rounds of speed bag and a full fifteen-minute period where Sensei just stood there and pegged me with water balloons for no real reason I could decipher, he shouted, "Take a knee!"

It was the least dangerous command he'd ever given me, but it was Sensei so I still bent down slowly, cautiously each moment thinking it could be the moment for a surprise spin kick. But no kick came. And then I saw something I never thought I'd see. The rubbery veins in Sensei's neck receded. His eyes sunk back into the normal, non-crazed position where eyes are supposed to sit, and his face softened from outright steel to something a bit softer. Like granite.

"Toby," he said, which was weird because he used my actual name and didn't attach any baked goods to it. "You have too much potential in the ring to waste time eating donuts and having a powdered sugar mustache. You understand?"

"I think so," I said.

"One way to know if you don't understand is you'll see me crouched down behind you, haunting you, just itching to give my new spin-kicking shoes another spin."

"I definitely understand," I told him, and I'd never been more sure of anything in my life. What I definitely understood without the slightest shred of a doubt was I'd rather do a little fake wrestling than have Sensei popping out of random trash cans all over Mapleton armed with a whole lot more spin kick than I'm willing to accept.

I guess it's back to practice on Monday. Great.

Wednesday, March 6

MAKING A SACRIFICE ISN'T all that fun.

There, I said it. And I'm still standing here without a single bolt of lightning flashing anywhere near me.

I said it because it's true. Take my week so far. Nothing but sacrifice. First, I went back to wrestling practice in an effort to save what's left of the El Machina spirit from the bony grips of Sensei and his some-of-you-may-die approach to training methods. That meant I had to sacrifice both my physical health (because SPOILER ALERT! I got my butt kicked every day. Weren't you listening?) to the fake wrestling gods and not even the real wrestling gods. The ones worshipped by actual luchadors like me and Dad.

But then I also had to sacrifice my sanity, because even though Mom hasn't shown up for any surprise "support" since the first practice, Coach Seam hasn't missed a session yet. I mean, he's the coach and all, so it's kind of his job, but I still have to see the guy more times in a day than I'm willing--and most of those times I'm lying flat on my back with another wrestler's boot on my neck. And, most of those times, it's a wrestler half my size with said boot on said neck.

So, like I said, it's a sacrifice. And I'm not really having a whole lot of fun with it (see: none). In fact, it's not even just at practice anymore where I do most of the sacrificing. Pretty much the hallways at Mapleton Middle, the cafeteria, most of the classrooms, and even the bathroom are now fair game for excruciating torture.

Those are some of the places where I sacrifice my pride, overhearing wimps like Jimmy Baker tell tea-spillers like Mandy Mallomar--and any other student who would listen (see: all of them)--about how he pinned me in less than ten seconds at the end of

Monday's practice (which was not true! It was actually ten point four seconds).

And, this morning. Boy. Just this morning I found an anonymous note stuck to the door of my locker. I opened it to find a bunch of wacky drawings that depicted me oozing across the wrestling mats like a puddle of mud and the rest of the team splashing around in me and laughing their stupid, little heads off. Talk about sacrifice.

I mean, if it wasn't such a sacrifice, I might even find the drawing clever. I might even think I deserve it for all the crappy things I did to my classmates in El Paso. But instead, I mope around school with my battery half charged. And that battery's planted firmly inside my brain. Or maybe it's in my heart. Or both. I can't tell.

All I can say is this whole Mom and Coach Seam thing is messing up my life, and even my future wrestling career, which is totally unacceptable to El Machina. It got so bad I can't even concentrate on a stinking Quadrant campaign anymore without hearing that sickening giggle--Mom's--somewhere off in the back of my mind.

That's why I decided to confront Coach Seam today after practice. He was busy folding up the wrestling mats and stacking them against the wall under the visitors' side basketball hoop. Mr. Finkelstein was already downstairs in the locker room, probably giving the rest of the team one of his patented pep-talks that mostly consisted of two or three words like, "Go get 'em!" or something even more generic.

I figured this would be my best chance to get Coach Seam alone and let him know what was what. Like, how I'm now the man of the Solano household and, oh, well I don't know where I was going with that.

All that really happened was I walked up to him and said, "Coach?"

And he was like, "How's it going, Toby?"

"Can I talk to you about something?" I asked.

And he was all, "Sure. You need to stagger your steps more before you attack, and it's important that you get more torque in your legs when you attempt a lift and if you try to--"

That's where I stopped him and said, "It's not about wrestling."

"Oh," he said, and his eyes shot down to the hardwood floor for a moment before he took a seat on the stack of sweaty, wrestling mats. He slapped a spot next to him with the palm of his hand. "Why don't you sit down," he said to me.

I sat across from Coach Seam and he let out a long, nasally exhale that told me he might already know what I was there to say to him. Almost like he was bracing himself for the worst, like I'd hit him with a flying tornillo from the top rope if he didn't say what I wanted to hear. And, for the record, I wasn't sure what I wanted to hear. Maybe that old Seam was leaving Mapleton to go coach wrestling in Uruguay or something.

Or maybe that my mom and dad weren't over forever.

"So, what can I do for you?" Coach Seam asked, even though I was pretty sure he knew what I would ask him.

"It's about my mom," I said. "You know, Cait Solano?"

"Yes, Toby. I know who your mom is," he said, fighting hard not to laugh, which was good because if he had it may have cost him a few teeth. "I guess you may have seen us together a few times in the past couple of weeks."

"More than a few times," I told him. "In the hallways, and at practice, and on her phone at all hours of the night, and--"

"Toby, slow down," he said. He dropped one of his hands down on my shoulder and stared at me for a few seconds with this look that said, "I get it." Then he nodded and continued. "I know what you're going through, Toby. When I was twelve years old, I lost my mom. She had pancreatic cancer and my father and I watched her fade away when she was only forty-two years old. We were heartbroken for a long time after she was gone. But people have to move on and, after a year or two, my dad started having this other woman--Linda--over for dinner once a week. It really bothered me, you know? It was like--"

"She was trying to replace your mom?"

"Exactly. And I couldn't deal with it. I stopped talking to my dad unless I absolutely had something critical to tell him, which was almost never, and I let myself feel sad and angry the rest of the time."

"What did you do?"

"Nothing," he said. "Just waited and let time take over, and eventually I got used to things being new. See, I kept trying to convince myself that life without Mom was the worst thing that could ever happen. But then I realized it was just different."

"And whatever happened to what's-her-name?" I asked. "Linda. How'd you get rid of her?"

This time Coach Seam didn't try to stifle his laugh. Then he said, "I didn't. She actually bought me these shorts I'm wearing for Christmas. Her and Dad will be married seventeen years in October."

It was a sweet story, don't get me wrong, but it also made my stomach churn in that terrible way it does when you're on a rollercoaster or if you just ate a truckstop burrito. I mean, I didn't know what to say to the guy after he basically told me to move on and forget about Dad--who I might mention is still alive and well, and will probably be making his pro-wrestling comeback any day now if I know him at all. So I sat there for a second and let a droplet of sweat roll off my temple and down the side of my face and into the collar of my t-shirt.

I pretended it was a tear, because I wanted to cry at that moment, to break down right there and flood out the whole gym with all the crud I've been storing inside me since Dad left. But I didn't want to let my wrestling coach see me cry after watching me get my butt smeared across the mat all practice. So I sat there and waited for Coach Seam to leave, which he did not.

Instead he said, "Look, I only told you that story to help you understand things won't always feel this way for you. You won't be sad

or angry or lost forever. Things will get better."
Then he gave me a playful slap on the back.
"Now, about your mom and me. We're friends,
Toby. Friends who work together and happen
to be facing similar obstacles in life. That's all.
I'm not here to replace your dad or steal your
family from you. I'm here to teach you how to
wrestle."

My ears perked up when he said it and at
least ten thousand pounds of weight lifted from
my shoulders. I smiled, and Coach Seam smiled,
and then he said, "We good?"

"We're good," I told him. I felt better. I never
thought in a million years Coach Seam would

be the guy to make me
feel like my life isn't
over, but I guess sages
and wizards can come
in many forms. Even in
the form of a middle-
aged gym teacher who
wears the dorky shorts
he got from Linda.

Sunday, March 10

IT WAS GOOD TO be in the same room as Mom this weekend and not feel like I was meeting someone for the first time. Like, we hit a ten-point-oh on the awkward scale the second she waved at Coach Seam in the gym, and nothing in my life has been normal since.

Yesterday morning, we stayed in our pajamas and cuddled under blankets to eat our bowls of Sugar-Ohs and watch reruns of *Tom & Jerry* cartoons. Mom loved Jerry the mouse, so I never bothered to tell her I feel kind of bad for Tom the cat because he tries so hard, and the only payment he gets in return is a face full of boiling water, or an Everest-sized knot on his head after a smash from a croquet mallet. I mean, the poor guy never gets a square meal. After at least four million episodes, there's never fresh mouse on the menu. The dude must be starving!

Starting the conversation was a dangerous and grueling task, much like walking a tightrope over a pit full of angry rattlesnakes, but it was something I had to accomplish if I was ever going to be happy. Or if I didn't want to feel like this forever.

"Mom," I said during a commercial for some fast food joint that was selling a burger in the shape of Pi for Pi Day, "do you and Dad still talk?"

My question caught her by surprise and a stream of milk dribbled down her chin into her cereal bowl. "Of course," she said. "Toby...of course I still talk to your father."

I was kind of nervous, so I rattled off questions before I lost the nerve. "When will we see him again?" I asked. "Where is he now?" and "Are we ever going back to El Paso?"

"Slow down, Toby!" Mom managed through a mouth full of Sugar-Ohs. She laid her spoon down in the bowl and placed the bowl on the coffee table. Then she picked up the remote and flicked the 'power' button on the TV. She pulled her blanket all the way up to her chin so only her face was visible above a wrinkled pile of fabric. "Your father is still in Mexico City. With *Abuelita*. He's training, Toby. You know that."

"But is he any closer?" I asked. "To his big comeback and... you know... to coming home?"

"I can't answer those questions," she said. "But I can tell you where home is. It's right here in Mapleton." I didn't like the sound of that, so I picked my empty bowl off the table and began to walk it to the dishwasher--anything to be out of that room without having to say what was really in my head. That I'd never consider this town my home, and Dad wouldn't either. That maybe he's the smart one out of the three of us for heading to Mexico instead of wasting his time in Mapleton. But I didn't say any of that. I didn't have a chance, because Mom jumped in before I could make my escape.

"I said I couldn't answer those questions for you," she told me, "but I think there might be someone who could." She ripped a long scrap off the corner of an old magazine and scribbled something on it. She handed it to me.

It was a phone number.

"I'm not trying to keep you from your dad," she said. "If you ever want to talk to him, all you have to do is dial." I pulled out my phone and programmed the number under the name 'Carisma, E", and then I let my finger hover over the 'call' icon, just for a second or two.

But then I slid the phone back in the pocket of my basketball shorts (don't judge me on my athletic pajama choices!) and sat back down next to Mom. I guess I wasn't ready to talk to Dad yet. I mean, what would I even say to him? I'd have to figure that out first.

Of course, figuring out what I might say to Dad one day far in the future when I finally get brave enough to grill a professional wrestler (a real one) on his life and career choices, would be much easier than what I faced at Zeke's Gym this morning.

Sensei was in rare form. When I pushed

through the front door, his face was already raging like a five-alarm fire, and the veins in his neck were a strong breeze away from complete explosion. Even so, the session began like any other, with Mr. Finkelstein and I running through the usual battery of all-out, muscle assault. First, there were rope climbs, and then medicine ball relays, followed by headbutt practice--all while getting pounded by a never ending stream of water balloons, which I'm pretty sure has little to do with training at this point, and everything to do with Sensei keeping himself amused at our expense.

But then Sensei disappeared into the caverns of the locker room before our usual sparring sessions at center ring. "Hop up here," Mr. Finkelstein said to me when he was sure Sensei's torture session was complete. I followed him under the ropes and into the center of Zeke's dilapidated practice ring.

"What are we doing?" I asked when it seemed like Mr. F had no plan.

"A little something extra," he said. "For the

Mapleton Muskrats."

I could feel my lips fold into a frown the moment he said 'Mapleton Muskrats'. "We're not gonna do that fake wrestling stuff here, are we?"

"We most certainly are," he said. "You could use the extra work, and it might even save your life."

"How's fake wrestling gonna save my life?"

"Not, like, from a natural disaster or anything," he said. "I mean your personal life."

"Wha-whaddya mean?" I didn't want him to hear the waver in my voice, which meant I knew that he knew that I knew...that he knows about all the abuse I've been putting up with from my teammates since my fake (and quite crappy) wrestling career began.

But I'm pretty sure he heard the waver anyway because he said, "Sometimes the best way to destroy a bully is to earn his respect."

"You mean beat the snot out of him?"

"No, Toby! I mean wrestling the snot out of him. Legally. On the mat at school."

"That hasn't exactly been working out for me," I told him.

"I know," he said. "I've been watching, and it hasn't been pretty."

"That bad?" I asked, and he didn't say anything which was probably worse than him just saying, "Yes, Toby, you're the worst. On the planet. Maybe the universe, and beyond."

"Doesn't matter," is what he actually said when he finally broke the silence and then he told me, "Give me twenty minutes and this week's practices will be a whole lot better for you than last week's."

I nodded, because what else was I going to do? Tell him he's crazy to believe in me and run screaming out the door like...well, like Big Baby (man, he sure comes up alot for such a forgettable wrestler).

That's when Mr. Finkelstein taught me the most important thing I'd ever learned about wrestling, fake or otherwise. Something that was so simple, but somehow more valuable than all the Lucha Libre moves Dad had taught me combined.

"The ground is your friend," he said.

"What are you talking about?" I asked. I mean, big boy fall down go boom is about the only thing that comes to mind when I think about the ground, and here is my English teacher trying to tell me it's my friend?

"In Greco-Roman wrestling, you need to keep a low center of gravity," he explained. "That means knees bent, body arched forward, so your opponent has to fight both you and the forces of the entire solar system."

"What?"

"It means you stay low to the ground, Toby. You know, so big boy don't go BOOM!" This I understood, and as I crouched around the ring in my new wrestling stance it suddenly dawned on me why Sensei forced me to do all that crab walking. Specifically for this purpose.

"Now, Toby, if you get taken down you can't panic. Again, use the--"

"Ground?" I asked. "My friend, right?"

"Exactly. What I do is pretend my mom is

trying to drag me out of bed in the morning, but I don't want to go to school."

"My mom never had to do that." "I said 'pretend'," he told me.

"Are *you* pretending, Mr. F?"

"Stop asking questions, Toby." I smiled at him and he shook his head.

"So, you mean I should make myself into dead weight?"

"Yes. Now you're thinking."

I laid on my stomach on the mat and made myself think like a massive sack of potatoes while Mr. Finkelstein tried to drag me to the other side of the ring or roll me over on my back. He couldn't do either, which kind of made me realize something:

The ground is my friend. No joke.

The whole lesson in gravitational force led Mr. Finkelstein to show me the proper stance and technique for a devastating leg snipe, adding "this will be one of your go-to moves," when I finally got it right on about the twentieth try.

And then he showed me how to use the

ground to my advantage again, with a move called the half-nelson, where I could anchor myself against the mat, slide my hand under my opponent's arm and lock it down like a viper on the back of the neck. I picked that one up quickly, and I can tell you I'll be using it the first chance I get. I hope it's on the Pitsniffer, if there are any wrestling gods out there listening.

Twenty minutes after the extra session began, I felt like a brand-new wrestler, just as Mr. Finkelstein had promised. I was thankful, because how often does someone give you a gift that helps you gain the respect of your teammates?

So I was like, "How about I repay the favor?

"What do you mean?" he asked. "These sessions are free of charge."

"I mean, you helped me look less like a fool on the fake wrestling mat...let me do the same for you in the ring."

"You think I look like a fool in the ring?"

"Not all the time," I said. "Only when you wear the Mort-tician's outfit."

"Gee, thanks."

"Come on," I said. "Let me show you another tough move."

"Lucha Libre style?"

"That's all I know," I said as Sensei emerged from the locker room and sat beside us on the apron of the ring. "I mean, I can't help it," I continued. "It's legacy."

"Legacy?" Sensei asked with his whole face suddenly lit up, and not in red this time.

"Yeah. My father is El Carisma, and so was his father, and his father's father. In Lucha culture it's common for a wrestling identity and all the moves developed by that luchador to be passed down through family lines. That means I was supposed to be the next El Carisma. I guess not anymore, which is fine because I'm already kind of set on a different name."

"What's that?" Mr. Finkelstein asked.

"El Machina."

"Ah," Sensei said lovingly. "The Machine. It's perfect."

"But I still learned a few of El Carisma's moves and I might as well pass them on to someone before the whole legend dies."

"I like that," Mr. Finkelstein said. "I have to tell you, I was about to say 'no way' to your idea, but how can I say that to a chance to be part of your tradition? Let's do it!"

We crawled under the ropes, and I had Sensei set up one of the extra heavy bags Zeke had lying around the gym.

"Umm...what is that for?" Mr. F asked when he saw it.

"Padding," I said in my best impression of Sensei Clement. "The move is called a double barreled *plancha.*"

"Plancha? What's that mean?"

"It means big boy go boom-boom off the top rope."

His lips curled back in fear. "And where does big boy go land-land?" I pointed to the downed heavy bag lying there on the cold cement. Then I climbed to the second rope and growled at the non-existent crowd like I knew only El Machina could. I stepped up to the top rope and gained my balance the way Dad had shown me, by wedging my heels against the turnbuckle. Then I went airborne in a perfect swan dive and crashed down on the heavy bag with both elbows, popping up unscathed from the wreckage with my beaten "opponent" lying lifeless on the cement.

It only took the Mort-tician two tries to learn the move. The second attempt yielded a perfectly executed double barreled *plancha* and a round of exuberant applause from both me and Sensei.

The first attempt, however, was a total fail

that I will not detail on the pages of this journal to protect the innocent (that would be Mr. Finkelstein) except to tell you it involved a poorly-timed misstep on the top rope, an awkward tumble into the center of the ring, and a strategically-placed wardrobe malfunction that I'll leave up to your imagination.

At least I know Mr. Finkelstein and I are prepared for another grueling week in the world of wrestling, whi Twenty minutes after the extra session began, I felt like a brand-new wrestler, just as Mr. Finkelstein had promised. I was thankful, because how often does someone give you a gift that helps you gain the respect of your teammates?

So I was like, "How about I repay the favor?

"What do you mean?" he asked. "These sessions are free of charge."

"I mean, you helped me look less like a fool on the fake wrestling mat...let me do the same for you in the ring."

"You think I look like a fool in the ring?"

"Not all the time," I said. "Only when you

wear the Mort-tician's outfit."

"Gee, thanks."

"Come on," I said. "Let me show you another tough move."

"Lucha Libre style?"

"That's all I know," I said as Sensei emerged from the locker room and sat beside us on the apron of the ring. "I mean, I can't help it," I continued. "It's legacy."

"Legacy?" Sensei asked with his whole face suddenly lit up, and not in red this time.

"Yeah. My father is El Carisma, and so was his father, and his father's father. In Lucha culture it's common for a wrestling identity and all the moves developed by that luchador to be passed down through family lines. That means I was supposed to be the next El Carisma. I guess not anymore, which is fine because I'm already kind of set on a different name."

"What's that?" Mr. Finkelstein asked.

"El Machina."

"Ah," Sensei said lovingly. "The Machine. It's perfect."

"But I still learned a few of El Carisma's moves and I might as well pass them on to someone before the whole legend dies."

"I like that," Mr. Finkelstein said. "I have to tell you, I was about to say 'no way' to your idea, but how can I say that to a chance to be part of your tradition? Let's do it!"

We crawled under the ropes, and I had Sensei set up one of the extra heavy bags Zeke had lying around the gym.

"Umm...what is that for?" Mr. F asked when he saw it.

"Padding," I said in my best impression of Sensei Clement. "The move is called a double barreled *plancha*."

"Plancha? What's that mean?"

"It means big boy go boom-boom off the top rope."

His lips curled back in fear. "And where does big boy go land-land?" I pointed to the downed heavy bag lying there on the cold cement. Then I climbed to the second rope and growled at the non-existent crowd like I knew only El Machina

191

could. I stepped up to the top rope and gained my balance the way Dad had shown me, by wedging my heels against the turnbuckle. Then I went airborne in a perfect swan dive and crashed down on the heavy bag with both elbows, popping up unscathed from the wreckage with my beaten "opponent" lying lifeless on the cement.

It only took the Mort-tician two tries to learn the move. The second attempt yielded a perfectly executed double barreled *plancha* and a round of exuberant applause from both me and Sensei.

The first attempt, however, was a total fail that I will not detail on the pages of this journal to protect the innocent (that would be Mr. Finkelstein) except to tell you it involved a poorly-timed misstep on the top rope, an awkward tumble into the center of the ring, and a strategically-placed wardrobe malfunction that I'll leave up to your imagination.

At least I know Mr. Finkelstein and I are prepared for another grueling week in the world of wrestling, which is more than I can say about his athletic shorts.

Thursday, March 14

– Pi Day π

SO… YEAH. THIS WEEK hasn't turned out the way I thought it would. At least, not on the wrestling mat. I mean, I tried to keep my center of gravity as low as it could go without being somewhere in the basement of the school, and I guess that wasn't low enough. On Monday, Jimmy whipped my legs out from under me and used the very same half-nelson to pin me that I planned to use on him. Thanks alot, wrestling gods.

On Tuesday, Derek spun around me and twisted my arm so far behind my back I thought it would come out the other side. Like, I totally thought I'd have to live the rest of my life with two left arms. So I tapped out. That means I forfeit. It was humiliating.

I tried to keep it all crammed down inside me, so I didn't have to think about my wrestling failures when I was anywhere else but on the mat, but by yesterday's lunch my anger was on the verge of going nuclear. Maybe the only thing that calmed me down (and only as a calm before the storm) was when Maya walked up to my table and plopped down her tray.

"Why do you look extra pathetic today?" she asked.

"Don't bother me," I said. "I'm busy." She stared at the unopened, brown bag of lunch that sat in front of me untouched.

"Yeah, you look swamped," she said. "I never saw hands move that fast. You're like Bruce Lee."

"Shut up," I said.

She pushed her glasses up on her nose and popped a cheese curl in her mouth, and I'm pretty sure she had this wicked, little grin on her mouth even as she chewed. "Come on," she said. "What's wrong?"

"You haven't heard? Jimmy Baker hasn't

spread it all over school yet?"

"About you sucking at wrestling? Oh yeah, I've heard that one already. But, who cares?"

"Who cares? Who CARES? Wrestling is my life, Maya. Now...how can that continue to be true if I get my butt kicked by the world's only living stick figure?"

"Because it's coming from Jimmy Baker," she said. "He talks so much the words all start to lose meaning. Besides, I'm sure it's not all that bad."

"Oh, it's bad."

Her eyes popped open a little and her head tilted back like she wasn't expecting me to be in agreement with the Pitsniffer. "How bad?" she asked.

"Bad," I told her.

"Like...how?"

"Like, I spent the whole week and most of last week floundering around on the mat like...well, like the world's biggest flounder. That's how bad."

"Eesh," she said under the cover of her

cheese curls, but I heard it and I knew it meant she probably thought I was a complete loser already, so I might as well tell her the rest.

"And then there's the drawings," I said.

"Drawings?"

"Yeah. Let's just say they're of me, not being the greatest wrestler of all time."

"Eesh," she said. Again. So why not keep painting the picture for her...or, better yet, the portrait. The portrait of a loser.

"The drawings were just taped to my locker last week, but now they're in my locker, in my bookbag when I unzip it after school, and even stuck to the back of my shirt if I don't walk past a mirror every ten minutes."

"Eesh." She made it again. That sound of pity, and the third time was enough to knock some sense into me. To stop feeling sorry for myself (like Maya had told me before), and to start asking what 'Tubby' Solano would do in a situation like this.

"I'm fed up," I said to her. "I've had enough of trying to play by Mr. Finkelstein's rules, trying to win respect on the mat. It's time to stop being a sucker, Maya, and put an end to this Baker business today."

"Oh yeah?" she said with a goofy grin on her face. "What tricks do you have up your sleeve?" When I didn't respond and, instead, stared straight past her on a laser beam path with Jimmy's table, her smile faded, and she knew I wasn't joking. "Toby," she said in a much lower tone and without the goofy grin. "No." I stayed silent and staring, and Maya sprang up from her chair without warning.

She grabbed her tray and said, "You're on your own," and then she left me sitting there in a familiar position. Alone.

It was a perfect opportunity for the moment, because I had an idea that would blow Jimmy Baker out of the water and take advantage of some nifty sketch work of my own. I mean, you may have noticed I like to doodle, so I figured why not take advantage of my hidden skills and prank the snot out of Jimmy Baker at the same time. The Pitsniffer would never know what had hit him.

So, I spent the rest of the lunch period eating my sandwich and sketching up this flyer:

I snagged Ms. Gluten's key to the library copy room from the key ring she always keeps on her desk, and I fired off a quick hundred or so copies and had the key back on the ring before Ms. Gluten was done shelving books in the dark recesses of the periodicals section (that's magazines and stuff for you laypeople). By the time I walked through the front door of my house and sat down to eat enchiladas with Mom, the entire sixth grade hallway, much of the school yard, and at least eighty percent of the storefronts in Mapleton were plastered with the signs. I imagined, right at that moment, the phone was ringing off the hook at the Baker household.

I also knew Mr. Baker from his very loud and very noticeable visits to watch his son practice wrestling. He didn't seem like the type of father who'd let his son off the hook if the whole town had paper evidence that Jimmy had offered up his services out of the kindness of his good, wittle heart--even if he'd never been aware of making the offer in the first place.

That's why today's lunch was a whole lot better (see: more entertaining) than yesterday's. Because today I stood in line behind Pitsniffer and listened to his whole conversation with Derek Meeks. First of all, the kid looked like he hadn't slept in days--years maybe--and there was a faint scent of grass and gasoline wafting off him.

Then I heard him say, "You can't believe it. I mowed every lawn on my street. It was dark, Derek! I was out there with a flashlight attached to my dad's mower and I never even got to plant Mrs. Pollena's bulb garden!"

His voice went all high-pitched and squealy when he said the words 'bulb garden', so it sounded more like 'buLB GARDen!' I guess I wasn't expecting it, or maybe it was the image that shot through my mind of Jimmy on his hands and knees, sobbing into a bag of tulip bulbs while his dad stood behind him holding the flashlight that did it.

But I laughed. Really, it was more of a snort, but it was bad. Because it gave me away, and in less than the time it took him to pin me during Monday's practice, Jimmy was able to put two and two together--so don't let anybody tell you Jimmy Baker's not good at math. Not even him.

All he did was look over his shoulder and stare me down for as long as he figured it would take for Derek to think he was a tough guy (it was roughly six point three seconds) and said, "This isn't over, Slow-bee."

Great. A prank war erupts, and I get a new nickname in the same day. At least 'Slow-bee' is a slight promotion over 'Tubby'.

Wednesday, March 20

THREE STRAIGHT LUNCH PERIODS sitting alone and an entire weekend of radio silence. Not a call. A text. Not even an email. That's how it's been between Maya and I since I told her I'd be pulling something over on Jimmy and then went out and turned the kid into Mapleton's one-man field crew. And it hasn't been my favorite period of time, watching the second hand tick...tick...tick by during lunch and having no one to talk to about how terrifying it is to live life knowing any moment could be the moment Jimmy chooses to unleash his revenge—in whatever barbaric form that may take.

I guess Maya doesn't understand how it feels to lose over and over again at the one thing you thought you were good at (wrestling) and then come to school each day and lose there too. That's why I did it. Why I couldn't stop myself from carrying out the cruel deed and then sitting back and enjoying the view. I mean, all I needed was a victory, and I got one.

But it was short-lived. As usual.

At first (see: today at lunch), the whole ordeal came with another small victory. Maya plopped her tray down and started eating. Like nothing had happened between us last week. She didn't say anything at first, and neither did I. Most likely because I was a little bit shy and a whole lot terrified, but after she twisted the cap off her bottle and took a long sip of water, Maya was ready to get down to business.

"As much as it satisfies me," she said, "to see Jimmy Baker doing some actual work out of the goodness of his sweet, innocent, little heart...I mean, I give you big style points on this one because you actually came up with the idea on your own instead of lifting it off some TV show you probably watched and--"

"I get the point, Maya," I said in the middle of her sentence. "I shouldn't have done it."

"You...shouldn't have?"

"No. I needed a boost. Something to make someone else feel like pig slime for once instead of me. But it was wrong. I might even feel bad for the kid if I wasn't looking over my shoulder every two seconds expecting a pie to slam me in the face, or a toilet to explode on me."

"That's...well, that's mature of you. I'm actually kind of proud of you."

"Thanks," I said, like the mature gentleman I am. Then I reached into my lunch bag--because I've been on a real PB&J kick since my day in detention--and right away I could tell I was not holding a peanut butter and jelly sandwich. First of all, it was a lot messier than any sandwich I've ever held in my hand and, second, it smelled like no other sandwich in the history of humankind. At least not edible ones.

I pulled the 'sandwich' out of my lunch bag.

It was brown.

It smelled like the dumpster behind the pet store.

It was mushy.

And that's when I found out what--if it wasn't already painfully obvious--I was holdingin my hand right there at my usual lunch table in the middle of the Mapleton Middle School cafeteria. There happened to be a note attached (how thoughtful!) that read:

Dear Slow-bee,

Did U think i'd forget to 'pick up' a gift for U from one of my clients? Fresh from Mr. F's yard. Complimints of Fawkner. Thanx fer the yardwerk. NJOY!

> *Yer Fiend,*
> *Jimmy.*

Maya's eyes were the size of pumpkins behind her glasses. She clamped her nostrils shut between her thumb and forefinger. But it wasn't Maya's shock that gripped my attention. It was Pitsniffer, two tables away, with a dog-poo-eating grin on his face and my half-eaten PB&J raised in front of him like he was making a toast at a wedding.

I don't know how he managed to get inside my locker and switch out my lunch bag with his lunch bag of assorted goodies, but Jimmy Baker had somehow pulled off the nastiest, most disgusting, and worst smelling prank I'd ever seen. And there was only one way for me to respond.

I turned my eyes on Maya, who still hadn't taken her first breath since I fished Faulkner's funk out of my bag and said, "You do realize this means war, right?"

She had no response. I didn't expect one.

Monday, March 25

MAYBE ALL THOSE WATER balloons weren't meant to keep Sensei busy during our training sessions. Maybe his methods weren't as pointless and maniacal as they appeared.

This weekend, during our normal routine of physical extremity, I even managed to duck a few balloons between taking cranium shots from Zeke's resident speed bag. I think I may have even gotten quicker or lighter on my feet, or maybe just lighter in general because either the elastic band on my gym shorts is stretched out or those bad boys don't fit anymore. The whole thing dawned on me this afternoon, when I went to wrestling practice and completed it without making a disgrace of myself right there on the mat.

I managed to win my first practice match, and it couldn't have come against a better guy.

A Pitsniffer disciple of the highest order, one Derek E. Meeks. Disclaimer: I don't know if Derek really does have a middle name, but in my mind he does and it starts with an 'E' (and that 'E' stands for enabler). Here's how I knocked him around a bit (just for fun) before I pinned the turkey (that's right, you read it here first).

So, the match started with both of us in the 'referee' position. That means one wrestler crouches down on the mat (that was me) and the other moves in over the top (that was Derek). Coach Seam blew the whistle and the first thing I did was remember what Mr. Finkelstein had told me: the ground is my friend. I dropped straight to the mat and flattened myself against it like an eel, while Derek heaved and pushed and tugged at my legs and arms. But he couldn't move me. Not even an inch! I was like a massive boulder in the middle of Derek's path, and he huffed and puffed and sweated himself into a frenzy trying to roll me out of the way.

The result: Derek's strength melted away like a glob of butter on a hot pan while I lay there stretched out and rested on the pool deck of the wrestling world. And then I caught the back of Derek's ankle and flipped him on his back. He was panting and clearly out of gas, so I dragged him around the mat on his belly a few times so he wouldn't forget he was messing with El Machina even if it was just fake wrestling and not the real stuff. Then, all I did was wrench one of his arms behind his back in a grappling hold until the only choice he had was to roll over and fall right into an easy pin.

Derek's shoulder blades hit the mat.

Coach Seam's palm hit the mat.

And then Jimmy Baker's headgear hit the mat.

He had torn the contraption off his head the second he saw Derek in trouble, and he dropped the thing in awe when the match came to an unlikely end, with me as the victor.

You'd think me proving myself on the mat would have been enough to gain some respect as a teammate and maybe even put the old 'Slow-bee' nickname to bed right next to 'Tubby'.

And you'd think, now that Jimmy had a chance to get even with me by way of Faulkner's dogpile, that he'd ease up on me a bit. Maybe even accept that I'm in his class and on the team and move on with his life.

But not Jimmy. Nope, not old Pitsniffer Baker.

I think beating his little minion, Derek, only

made things worse between Jimmy and I because instead of whispering rude crap about me behind my back, he has graduated to saying those things directly to my face.

Like today, after practice. He waited for Coach Seam and Mr. Finkelstein to head down to the locker room and then he cornered me as I stacked the wrestling mats. "Don't fool yourself, Slow-bee," he said. "You got lucky. The tipped cow routine won't work on me."

I didn't want to get in an argument with the kid, but he just makes it so easy. So I said, "I have other moves."

"Oh yeah?" he spit back at me. "Like what? You gonna wheel in a mattress next time and lay on that?"

"Not a bad idea," I said. "I may consider it."

"Yeah, well I hope you enjoyed your lunch the other day, cause I went through a whole lot of trouble preparing it for you."

"It was great," I said. "Thanks." It was hard chewing back what I really wanted to say to Jimmy, but the nicer I was to him, the redder his face got and the more confused he looked, so I figured it couldn't hurt to be nice to the kid. Just this one time. I finished him off with, "My compliments on the note, Jimmy. Your spelling and grammar is always a special treat."

"Urrgh!" was the last thing he kind of said. It was more of a croaking noise in his throat combined with a moan and mixed with a grumble. Whatever it was, it didn't seem to make him happy because he turned and stormed off and all I could hear him whisper under his breath was the word 'loser'.

Hmmm. Loser. First 'Slow-bee' and now 'Loser'.

I guess you can't keep everyone happy all of the time, even when you're trying to be nice. I'm guessing 'happy' will be the last word anyone will use to describe Jimmy when he sees what I have in store for him next.

I mean, this *is* war after all.

Thursday, March 28

TODAY WAS ONE OF those rare days where it didn't matter what I did or how I did it, but everything was going to work out without a wrinkle, flaw, or even a scratch.

It was a perfect day for so many reasons, both important and insignificant. Like, I woke up exactly one minute before my alarm sounded and switched it off before I (or Mom, or anyone else in Mapleton) had to endure the daily eardrum shattering.

Then, I got called to the board during Mrs. Yance's first period math class, which wasn't great because I had no idea what to make of the random grouping of squiggles she wrote up there and insisted was an equation. I prepared myself for the worst as I filled in a bunch of random letters and numerals in the places she'd left blank. I think I may have inserted an @

symbol in there somewhere (I can't be sure).

But when I turned around and opened my eyelids from their instinctively defensive positions, Mrs. Yance smiled and broke into this slow, snooty applause (like the kind you see at a golf match) that apparently meant I'd done good. Potential humiliation averted, and I returned to my desk thinking I better pick some lottery numbers for Mom tonight.

After Math, I went to my locker and the perfect string of perfectness that was this perfect day (this rare and lovely day) continued perfectly when Maya pulled up as I was changing out my books. Normally, that's good in and of itself, but then she was like, "Great t-shirt, Toby. The Blue Demon?" which was cool because I'd never met anyone in Mapleton who'd ever heard of the guy, even though he's basically one of the most famous luchadors of all time.

"You know the Blue Demon?" I asked her, just to make sure.

She said, "Only that he weighed in at one hundred eighty-seven pounds, stood five feet seven inches, was nicknamed *El Manotas* because he had huge hands, and he finished off his opponents with a move called the octopus hold. But that's all. Nothing else."

I didn't say anything, because I didn't want to ruin one of the coolest moments of my life...which got a few degrees cooler when Maya and I walked into lunch and there was a surprise ice cream bar! For no reason at all, other than today was a perfect day.

Still, nothing put a cap on today like my performance during wrestling practice. It may have been my best one yet. First, we ran shuttle sprints on the basketball court like we do every day, and not only did I finish this time, but I also finished second; only a few steps behind the dripping wet Pitsniffer himself (more on that later).

After sprints, I beat the snot out of Derek Meeks again in a head-to-head match (this time on points after I wrapped him up in a sweet cradle move). So, there are no questions lingering about our last match being a fluke. It was not.

Finally, we broke into groups and ran through a bunch of speed and agility drills, none of which resembled anything I did with Sensei and Coach Fink down at Zeke's Gym. In fact, all of these Coach Seam-inspired drills were quite logical, obviously beneficial, and mostly non-lethal (which was a good change of pace from what I've grown used to).

After practice, Coach Seam pulled me aside

and didn't mention a word about Mom, and it didn't even feel the slightest bit awkward. He said, "Toby, you're making progress faster than I can chart it. You eating differently or something? Because you're lightning-fast out there lately."

I thought about the triple-dipped banana split I'd made myself in the cafeteria earlier and said, "Not really." I mean, did you want me to lie to the guy? I haven't changed a thing about my diet, unless you count the steady diet of water balloon torture I've been served daily by Chef Sensei. I doubt that counts.

Of course, I may have left out one part. One glorious and victorious part of my perfect day that will stay with me forever and give me goosebumps every time I think about how I pulled it off. How I got Jimmy Baker good this time.

What I did was simple. All it took was patience. I waited around in the locker room before wrestling practice until everyone was in the gym under the cover of playing waterboy (that means I volunteered to fill up the massive, team water jug for practice). When I say 'everyone' was in the gym, I really mean 'everyone minus one'. And wouldn't you know it? That 'one' happened to be Jimmy Baker.

I knew he'd be there because if there's one thing I knew about Jimmy that I desperately wished I didn't know, it was that he always had to 'make weight' before practice, which is a polite, wrestling way of saying you could find him in the jon making stinkies. Like I said, I wish I didn't know.

But since I did, I figured I'd use that little piece of information to my advantage. I filled up two water jugs today instead of one and scooped big piles of ice from the trainer's ice machine inside until the water was cold enough to give a polar bear hypothermia. One jug was for the team because hydration matters.

The other jug?

Well, that one got tipped over the stall that contained one Jameson 'Pitsniffer' Baker, until his clothes stuck to him like Saran Wrap and his hair was piled with ice cubes.

"I'll get you Solano!" was the last thing I heard as I bolted out of the locker room with the team's fresh supply of ice cold H20.

The poor kid looked like he'd run a marathon before wrestling practice when he showed up in the gym a few minutes later. He was drenched to the bone (see, I told you I'd get to it), and the three-foot section of air that surrounded him smelled faintly of toilet water. He wasn't happy, but I can tell you I was grinning ear to ear.

Man, you don't get days like this one too often. I guess I better enjoy the lift while it lasts. I'm sure the days ahead will be littered with Jimmy Baker-sized landmines from here on out.

Monday, April 1

– April Fool's Day

I'LL KEEP THIS ENTRY short because I'm too angry to sit around writing about it all night. I'm not even sure who I should be mad at?

Jimmy Baker? I mean, I kind of saw this coming after the Alaskan toilet trick I pulled on him last week.

Should I be angry at the dweeb who created April Fool's Day for starting a tradition that urges people to embarrass others in public? Nah. The date's written down on every calendar in the world, so it's my fault for letting it sneak up on me today. Should I be mad at myself? For falling for the lamest, most obvious prank in the history of April Fool's Day pranks?

Yes.

Yes, that's the one.

What happened was, I went to my locker

like I always do after Fink's class--just to change out books and waste a few minutes--and there was something waiting for me inside when I popped the door.

It was a small, rectangular box wrapped up in paper with a bunch of cartoony-looking insects printed on it. There were big, smiling ladybugs sitting atop a marigold bloom, and ants with hard hats and tool belts strapped to their segmented bodies. There were googly-eyed earthworms dripping with mud, and a quartet of crickets sawing out tunes on their fiddles.

It should have been my first clue that something was up. Something wasn't right. But I thought, maybe it's a gift from Maya. It was her kind of style with the geeky insects and all. Maybe she had heard about my recent heroics on the wrestling mat and she wanted to surprise me with something special.

So I opened it.

Right there in the hallway between Mr. Fink's classroom and the water fountain.

Big mistake.

The second the lid was off the box, a million tiny, hopping hellraisers sprang forth in a disgusting cascade of bulgy eyes and scrapey legs and creepy, crawly parts.

Crickets! And they were everywhere.

They bounced around the hall and held congress on the top shelf of my locker. They crawled up and down the front of my  bookbag and hopped and chirped and probably reproduced at a rate that would leave my locker (and maybe all of Mapleton) thriving with a cricket population worthy of the apocalypse.

I wasn't happy, and I'm sure I know whose grin was beaming ear to ear on this day. It definitely wasn't mine. But don't worry. I'm already three or four phases into my next plan of attack.

The one that will obliterate Jimmy Baker. For good.

Friday, April 5

IF THERE'S ANYTHING THAT can get your mind off revenge (at least, temporarily), it's a tough training session. And if there's anyone who could literally make you wish you were hiding inside your own locker (in the thick of cricket kingdom) instead of training, it's Sensei.

The circuits Sensei Clement set up for Coach Fink and I this week have been as ridiculous and painful as usual, but today's descent into the lava pit was somehow the peak of the man's brutality (I hope). Today's experience consisted of three, basic exercises—or, at least, that's what Sensei called them. 'Evil sorcery' seemed a bit more accurate to me.

The first thing Sensei did was blow into this screeching banshee of a whistle that even put Mom's annoying tea kettle to shame. But then he moved his hand from his mouth, and I noticed he hadn't been blowing into a whistle at all. Nope. The same sound that marked the start of our workout, and the same sound that made my ears want to melt off the side of my head, was a sound that only a man as hardened and disciplined as Sensei Clement could emit using only the two most skeleton-like fingers on his left hand and presumably some sort of a lizard tongue. I don't know, but I can tell you it got my attention to the point where I thought Coach Fink would have to peel what was left of me and my clothes off the rafters.

Before I had a chance to catch my breath, Sensei shouted, "Give me more kettle bell!" and he pulled out these two, orange batons from under his black belt--the kinds of batons controllers use to direct planes on a runway. "Relocate the weight!" he screeched, and Coach Fink and I lifted all seventy-three kettle bells (of assorted sizes and weights) from their normal position beside the water fountain to a free wall on the opposite side of the gym. The whole time Sensei barked orders at us, timed us on his stopwatch, reminded us we were "slower than stagnant puddles", and waved in each of our weighted-down flights with the whip of his airplane batons. It was madness!

He blew his "whistle" the second I dropped the final kettle bell in place and shouted, "Time to ride!" which technically had nothing to do with riding any one of the eight stationary bikes in Zeke's fleet and everything to do with the words, "Relocate the weight!" Which, again, meant simply that--lifting and wheeling each bike from its present position to the space by the water fountains once dominated by kettle bells...the whole time he clocked us, waved us in, and reminded us our top speed "was about the same as two dried-up boogers," which I assume was meant as a compliment, coming from Sensei.

He blew his mouth siren again and shouted, "Relocate the weight!" and this time it was literal. He actually made us take each plate off the free weight rack, move the rack to the space once occupied by stationary bikes, and then carry each plate one-by-one and replace them on the rack. The typical shouting and speed-related swipes at us came standard.

Then old Zeke himself stepped out of his office for a rare sighting of the closest human being I've ever seen to being an actual statue of himself. I mean, the dude was chiseled from granite, although I don't know when he ever gets a chance to do his workouts with all the sitting around in his office smoking the stinkiest cigars you've ever smelled in your life he's got going on.

Anyway, the second Coach Fink had the last twenty pounder set on the rack in its new position, Zeke looked around his gym and his mouth scrunched into that position it goes into when you smell spoiled milk. He said, "Nah. I don't like it." Just like that. And then he crawled back inside his office under a mushroom cloud of cigar smoke.

"Relocate the weight!" Sensei shouted.

It didn't dawn on me until the final kettle bell was replaced in its original position that today's circuit had nothing to do with training and everything to do with...interior decorating! That's right, Coach Fink and I were just moving all the "furniture" around Zeke's Gym like Sensei Clement's personal moving service! If you're picturing me right now, assume I'm in full facepalm formation.

But, you know, after I thought about it I realized maybe Sensei Clement's pointless demonstration of exercise cruelty had a point after all. Besides the rigorous exercise, I mean.

I think Sensei was trying to show us the importance of changing your perspective once in awhile. Just to stand back and see if the solution you've always been searching for might appear when you think there's no hope. He was showing us how to change our view, alter our strategies from the predictable and expected. I mean, I'm not sure if Sensei knew he was showing us any of that stuff, but it's what I took from the experience. That, and at least two days' worth of sore muscles in my future.

That's why I cut my closing session with Coach Fink short today after practicing our usual ropes routine and taking only a single practice splash off the top of the turnbuckle. My muscles were fine. It was something else that slowed me down and made my mind drift far away from the training ring. So, I stopped the session midstream, after Fink sent me running to the far ropes and, instead of bouncing back, I just held onto the top rope with both of my hands behind me--I'd seen the Fink do it once or twice, but it was really a move Dad taught me back in El Paso.

Coach Fink looked at me kind of funny, like he didn't know what his next move should be, and he said, "You okay, Toby? You pull a hamstring or something?"

"No," I said. "I'm fine." But I wasn't. And I told him everything because I needed to get it off my chest. About the prank war. About what I'd done to Jimmy and how he fought back (dirty, I might add). And about the wrestling team, and all the razzing I'd been taking because I'm still learning this whole fake wrestling thing.

"You don't want to get involved in that," Mr.

Finkelstein said.

"You mean a prank war?" I asked.

"Call it what you want. I call it a revenge cycle."

"That sounds like a pretty cool wrestling name," I said.

"I wish it were, Toby. But it's more like if a robot malfunctioned and got stuck in a loop, repeating the same function over and over again without reason and without helping anyone or anything in the process. You think you understand what I'm saying?" I nodded because I knew if I pulled another fast one on Jimmy it would only be like knocking down a single domino in a line of twenty million more dominoes to follow, and I just didn't have the time (or the energy) for any of that.

So, I've made a decision. I'm doing some interior decorating. Upstairs. In my head. Because it's time to change my perspective on this whole prank war thing before it gets (any more) out of control. I'm going to do something a hundred times better and at least a thousand times more courageous than any prank I could have pulled anyway.

I'm pulling the plug on the war.

Raising the white flag.

Calling it off.

And then I'm challenging Jimmy Baker to a fake wrestling match at our next practice, see if I can put an end to this stupid conflict in the only way I see possible. I guess if I ever get the guts to tell Sensei about it, he'd be proud. Or not.

Tuesday, April 9

OKAY, SO I MIGHT as well come right out with it: I didn't have the guts to challenge Jimmy at practice yesterday. All I did in class, and just about everywhere else, was think of ways to come flying out on the mat at practice and be like, "Aaaarrgh! Jimmy, you're going down!" or something even tougher that you might hear from a luchador to get the crowd united against an opponent.

But practice came and went, and the only thing I said to Jimmy was, "Pass me a cup," while we stood in line at the water jug, and he held out a cup and dropped it on the ground a second before I could grab it. I went home with nothing but the recent sting of the prank war humiliation hanging over me, and a few of my new cricket friends hitching a ride on my backpack.

It's probably why I couldn't sleep well, and why I stayed up half the night playing in about forty different campaigns of Quadrant. It's probably why I woke up feeling exhausted, and why I sat there at my lunch table staring at my PB & J sandwich with no intention of eating it, when Maya slammed her tray down next to me and said, "Would you stop moping around and just wrestle the kid already?" I'd sent her a text after Friday's training session and told her about my sudden change in perspective, and I guess it was written all over my face that I couldn't follow through.

"It's not that simple," I told her, and the eye roll she gave me from behind her massive spectacles was magnified to at least one hundred times.

"Look," she said, "I'm not gonna lie to you. Watching you two idiots humiliate each other is the most entertainment any of us get around this place. But, Toby, I'm tired of watching you drool all over your sandwich just because you're afraid to get in the ring and get it over with."

"It's a mat," I said. "Remember, this is fake wrestling we're talking about."

"Whatever," she said, but it was enough. I had to say, it was a decent pep talk. Of course, I didn't say that to her because the last thing I need is for Maya to go Knute Rockne on me each day at lunch, but she did get me fired up. As soon as practice started, I was like, "Jimmy Baker. Me and you. Mano e mano." All cold as steel, just like that.

No.

What really happened was I walked up to Coach Seam and asked if he would let me wrestle Jimmy, and he said, "A challenge?" I nodded. "I like it," he said. He blew his whistle and the whole team gathered around with me and Jimmy standing toe-to-toe at the center of the mat. Jimmy's eyes squinted shut. The corners of his mouth pitched upward in a sneer.

"You're dead," he mouthed to me, but no words came out so it was twice as chilling. My heart beat pounded in my eardrums. My skin prickled with all the eyes casting stares down on it. To be honest, I have no idea how I managed to keep my sandwich in my stomach where it belonged. I guess it was Coach Finkelstein, standing behind the rows of my teammates, that allowed me to chew it back. All it took was a slight nod that you'd only be able to notice if you happened to get hit with the same water balloon as the guy down at Zeke's Gym. Thankfully, I had.

That's when Coach Seam blew his whistle and the match was on. And it was weird, because as soon as I locked horns with my arch nemesis, everything around me faded into nothing. It just vanished and there was nothing left but me, the mat, and Jimmy Baker--which I guess you probably figured out from the whole "mano e mano" thing.

Jimmy didn't waste time. He crouched low to the ground with one foot slightly in front of the other, and he lunged at my ankles like a viper. Or maybe like a rogue water balloon, and all I did was jump over him--like a luchador potentially named El Machina.

Jimmy spun around about a second too late. I wrapped my arms around his waist and used my weight to drive him to the mat. "One point for the take down!" Coach Seam shouted with one slap of the mat.

From there, I had Jimmy right where I wanted him. On his back, inches away from the pin. And, to be completely honest, I couldn't believe it. I mean, here I'd been building this rematch up in my mind all weekend, thinking about how Jimmy had cleaned my clock in under ten seconds. How he'd humiliated me in front of the whole team and spread the news far and wide across the middle school. And now I had one of his shoulder blades pressed firmly on the mat and the other one just centimeters from Pinsville, USA.

But that was the exact moment my confidence decided to rebel against me.

That's when I looked up and caught the eyes of Derek Meeks and my teammates, and I smiled when I saw each one of their jaws dropped wide open in synchrony. It took less than a second, but it was all Jimmy needed to slither from my grasp like the slimy snake he is and roll to his feet. He dove on my back and pancaked me to the mat before I could take my next breath. "Two points, Baker!" Coach Seam shouted, and then the nail in the coffin a few seconds later, "TIME!"

That was it.

I'd lost to Jimmy.

Again.

And it sucked.

But then something crazy and cool and totally unexpected happened. Something I never thought was possible. Jimmy walked straight up to me in the locker room after practice and he didn't say, "You're a disgrace to wrestling," or "There might be a wrestler in you if you whittle away the blubber," or the simple, patented classic, "You stink, Slow-bee." This time he didn't say anything. He just held out his hand and waited for me to shake it.

I stared at him for a few seconds, because what in the world was he doing?

"Come on, Toby," he said. "Shake my hand. No funny stuff."

I reached out cautiously and we shook. Like, for real and not with any novelty hand buzzers involved or anything. "You might not stink as bad as I thought," Jimmy said, which was basically the highest compliment you can ever expect to get from a pitsniffer.

"Thanks," I said. "But I should have pinned you."

"You did," he said. "Except for the part where you felt sorry for me and let up."

"I don't know if I--"

"Let it go, Toby. Like, all of it."

"What do you mean?"

"Let's call truce," he said. "Maybe even be friends."

This time I held out my hand and waited for Jimmy to shake, which he did without hesitation.

"Of course," he said, "this means we have another problem."

Another problem? For the life of me, I

couldn't figure out what Jimmy was talking about. "What problem?" I asked. "I thought a truce meant we're good."

"We are good," he said. "It's Coach Finkelstein who's anything but good right now."

"What do you have against Coach?"

"Nothing. I want to help him. I know you think I love tearing up the guy's classroom every day, but even that gets old after awhile. He needs to get on track. He needs to wrestle again." I nodded. "From what I hear around town," he continued, "you two are training together, so you must want to help too."

I couldn't believe I was in agreement with Jimmy Baker on something, but he was right: I did want to help Mr. Finkelstein. But more than that, I wanted to help the Mort-tician. "You do realize what you're saying?" I asked.

"I'm saying we're teammates, so let's act that way. Let's get the Mort-tician back in the ring."

"I'm in," I say.

"And this time, no baby stuff. We get him to

fight for the title or nothing."

We shook on it (for, like, the third time today), so I'm pretty sure that means our pact is indestructible.

Friday, April 12

WE WAITED ALL WEEK for the perfect time, to catch him at his most vulnerable—as soon as class ended, and he needed to rush to the teachers' lounge for his next cup of coffee. That's when the most unlikely group of heroes—me, Maya, and Jimmy Baker—embarked on our mission, which Maya unofficially codenamed 'Operation: Let Me Do All The Talking" when she told us before class, "You guys should really let me do all the talking."

Jimmy and I agreed with her, but once the clock struck noon and our classmates filed out, the whole operation—which was supposed to be the three of us cornering Mr. Finkelstein behind his desk and Maya rattling off all the reasons he should try to reclaim his title (see: laying a thick guilt trip on him)—turned into the three of us circled around Mr. F's desk like a starving gaggle of roadside vultures, and our teacher was the roadkill. Then we fired off questions at the basic popping rate of a battery of Black Cat firecrackers.

"You've been training hard," I said.

"And you're in better shape now than when you were champ," Maya told him.

"And you're smarter now," Jimmy said, "because of all your experience."

"Plus, you have moves and a different style," I said.

"And there's still time to learn more," Maya added.

"Yeah," Jimmy said, "you won the belt before without knowing a thing."

"Besides," Maya said, "do you want people to remember the Mort-tician for that retirement party of a match you fought last month?"

"Yes," I said. "You have a responsibility to honor your sport and your identity."

"It's, like, written in stone," Jimmy said. "We don't make the rules, Mr. F."

"And what would your mother think if she

knew you were giving up so easily?" Maya asked with an edge in her voice all of a sudden. "Huh, Norbie?" Wow. The girl fought dirty, and her hard-nosed tactics produced the first crack in Mr. Finkelstein's armor. Up to that point he'd been staring straight ahead with a frown on his face and an empty coffee mug dangling from his index finger.

But then he placed the mug firmly on his desk. Not a slam, but loud enough to let us know our firing squad routine had been issued a cease-fire. "Don't bring my mother into this fantasyland idea you all have for me," he said. "Truth is, I don't want to get in the ring with The Champ or anyone else."

"But you said--"

"Doesn't matter, Toby," he said. "I know you think the belt is what I want and I may have even believed you, but now I'm not sure. I'm happy I was able to get in there one more time and prove I could wrestle if I had to."

"You call that match against Selfie Stick Saul proving yourself?" Maya asked.

"Yeah," Jimmy said, "I heard it looked more like you were sparring against your neighborhood mailman."

"It's time for me to pack away the Morttician suit, Jimmy. I have nothing left to fight for. Mom saw Greece. Valerie and I are happy. Why get flattened for nothing?"

"For nothing?" I asked, and I couldn't believe my ears because if there was one person in this town I thought lived and breathed wrestling--like, REAL wrestling--as much as I did, it was Mr. F.

I guess I was wrong.

"Besides, I doubt I can survive an entire match against The Champ," he added, "let alone beat him."

And that's when we our shoulders dropped and walked out of Mr. Finkelstein's classroom with our tails between our legs-- which was just another way of saying our newfound teamwork didn't achieve squat.

It felt so weird and awkward after our big fail that Jimmy and I instinctively sulked off in opposite directions the moment we hit the hallway. But then we heard it. "Where are you two clowns going?" Maya asked over the rush of passing hallway traffic. That stopped Jimmy and me in our tracks.

"What do you want to do now?" I asked, my frustration oozing out of every syllable.

"You heard the guy," Jimmy said. "He doesn't want to wrestle. What are we supposed to do? Hoist him up in a giant crane and lower him into Mapleton Auditorium?"

"I guess we need to face it," I said, "and say our goodbyes to the Mort-tician."

The glasses slid down the bridge of Maya's nose and I knew we were in for it. "We're not giving up like that," she shrieked. Then she smiled--that glorious, treacherous, whimsically mischievous kind of smile that always precedes a statement like, "Besides...I have an idea."

Maya always has an idea. Let's hope this one--whatever it may be--is as brilliant as all the rest. For the sake of the Mort-tician's honor, and for Mr. Finkelstein's passion. And to restore my faith in a surprising hero, and maybe keep the wrestling gods happy for one more day.

Monday, April 15
– Tax Day

EVER HEAR THAT STUPID saying, "The only things you can count on are death and taxes?" I mean, I'm too young to pay taxes, but I can tell you there are many more things you can count on in life. Like your parents, or burning the roof of your mouth when the pizza's too hot, but you just can't wait.

And there's Maya.

You can count on Maya for more things than I could list in ten  volumes of this journal. Like, she'll never be late to anything in her life, and she'll always appear out of thin air to save your sorry butt, and (the most important of all) she'll always have a plan.

And it will work.

Like, always.

Take today, for example. Jimmy and I spent the weekend texting back and forth with different ideas (see: schemes) we could pull on Mr. Finkelstein to convince him to challenge The Champ and win back his respect. The best we came up with was to blindfold the guy and tell him we're bringing him to a surprise party in his honor (which wouldn't have been much of a surprise, geniuses) and, instead, we'd deliver him to center ring at Mapleton Auditorium where The Champ and ten thousand fans would be sitting there waiting for a match to stir up out of nowhere.

We scrapped the idea when we realized the only two things we could count on were poor Finkie either passing out on the spot or straight up dropping dead from fright the second the blindfold came off. Neither option seemed promising and, after that, the braintrust between Jimmy and I was completely tapped.

We had nothing.

No. We had less than nothing.

But when we sat down at our normal table in the cafeteria (today, Jimmy started sitting with us) Maya said, "Meet me at this address after practice." She plopped two identical scraps of paper down in front of Jimmy and me. The words '1127 Oak Street' were printed on each one. Then she got up and left before either of us could ask a question.

She didn't buy lunch or anything. In fact, I didn't see Maya for the rest of the school day, which was weird because we started this habit of visiting each other's lockers between classes (mostly I visit her locker since the crickets built an apartment complex in mine).

When I showed up at 1127 Oak Street with Jimmy two steps behind, it became clear why Maya had gone AWOL. She'd been recruiting some kind of thug, or henchman, or maybe a hitman (I couldn't tell). She stood in front of a brown door, on the porch of an ordinary-looking bungalow, on an ordinary street with the least ordinary person I've ever seen standing beside her. The guy was dressed in leather from head to toe, and he wore a weird cap on his head with a shock of curly hair as bushy as a fox tail exploding from the back. Every visible part of his body was claimed by some kind of gaudy jewelry, from rope chains to bracelets to matching, pinkie rings.

I was confused at first and, judging by the look on Jimmy's face, I could tell he was taking in the same view as me. I mean, did Maya actually leave school today to hire a gangster to threaten our English teacher into a wrestling match? It didn't sound like Maya, and yet here we were standing in front of the brown door, on the ordinary street, with a guy who may have double-crossed Al Capone.

But then the guy started to speak, and I could tell right away Maya's plan was a stroke of genius. It didn't involve threats of any kind, but it did involve a healthy dose of trash talk.

First, Maya introduced us. "Toby, this is the well-known wrestling promoter, Joseph Happenstance."

"Please," he coughed out in a gravelly voice,

"call me Joey. That's what my friends call me." He held out his hand. I saw no reason not to shake it, other than a slight fear of getting my fingers trapped between his arsenal of rings like hot dogs in a garbage disposal.

Jimmy, on the other hand, turned around and crossed both arms over his chest. He refused to speak or even look at the guy, as if they had some kind of ancient grudge between them.

"Baker," Joey grunted without really looking at Jimmy, and while puffing up a curiously thin spot on his hair explosion.

"They've met," Maya said. "But don't ask them about it."

"Why are we here, Maya?" I asked. I mean, someone had to say it.

"Mr. Happenstance is The Champ's representative," she said. "And a master of negotiations." She winked at me, and I had no clue what it was supposed to mean.

"I'm a master of most things," Happenstance said. "That includes putting weary, old wrestling no-bodies to rest. It's my specialty." Jimmy grunted something I couldn't make out, but it didn't sound like a compliment. Maya smiled at me like a cartoon character, and I felt this burning twinge inside me that I didn't like. Because it told me I knew what this Happenstance bozo was getting at, and I didn't like him bad-mouthing the Mort-tician right in front of me.

And just as I was about to fire back something lethal at Joey Happenstance...I stopped myself. Let the words pile up in the back of my throat and swallowed them in one whole sentence. Because I realized this was it. This was Maya's plan.

Right on cue, Maya pounded on the door and who do you think answers? Yep. It's Mr. Finkelstein. The Mort-tician. And I could tell right away he was standing toe-to-toe with his nemesis--the man he despised most in life. Joey Happenstance.

"Why did you bring him here?" Mr. Finkelstein said to Maya with both of his eyeballs leaping out of his head.

"Just hear him out," Maya said, which was the only opening Happenstance needed to run his scheme.

"Norbie!" he shouted, as if greeting a long, lost relative. "You look great as always. Like you couldn't wrestle a stray cheese doodle back into the bag, my friend. Or maybe you didn't want to! Right? Am I right?"

"What do you want, Joey?" Mr. Finkelstein said. The last bits of his patience oozed out of him with each word.

"Me?" Joey asked, like he hadn't come here to start trouble. "I don't want nothing...but the chance to remind you that I have your belt and you're never getting it back."

"I don't want it back," Mr. Finkelstein said.

"Come on," Joey said. "It's me, Norbie. You can be honest with me. You can trust me."

"Leave, Joey."

"What's your problem, Finkel-face? You mean to tell me if I gave you a chance to win back your belt, you'd be too afraid to take it?"

"Leave now, Joey."

At that moment, the door swung open a little wider and a lady with a gentle smile and a swoosh of white hair stood next to my teacher in the doorway. "What's this, Norbie?" she asked. "You have visitors?"

"It's nobody, Mom," Mr. Finkelstein said. Maya, Jimmy, and I didn't move a muscle. In fact, the only muscle that happened to be moving (lucky for us) was Joey's mouth.

"Ohhh, I see now," he said with a jagged sneer rising on his face. "Mommy don't want little Norbie-pooh to fall down and get a boo-boo."

The Mort-tician's eyes narrowed and his top lip curled up and started to quiver. A bead of sweat squeezed from a pore on his forehead and rolled down his face. He turned and took one look at his mom's face, which had suddenly become as chiseled and hardened as her son's. She gave him a nod, and the Mort-tician reached out and grabbed Joey Happenstance by the collar of his white t-shirt and pulled his face to within an inch of his own.

"You'll have your match, Happenstance. Name the date and the time. I'll be there." He released his grip on Joey's shirt and let him flop on the seat of his pants. Happenstance popped up and dusted himself off. He smirked and said, "Always a pleasure, Norbie." Then he was gone.

I don't know if I'd call the experience a pleasure, but Maya's plan worked. We've got ourselves a title match. With The Champ. And, finally, it's something we can count on.

Thursday, April 18

WE STARTED TRAINING THE Mort-tician today for his big match, which is set for May 12—Mother's Day. I guess Happenstance was trying to be cute when he just happened to pull that date out of his funny, little hat. You know, by pure Happenstance.

I mean, school was the same old thing, and practice has been, well, practice. But the Mort-tician's training session this afternoon was a thing of beauty. And, mostly, that's because I didn't have to run the circuit with him. Sensei made me an honorary member of the Mort-tician's training staff, which meant I got to skip all the torture my poor English teacher went through today.

Sensei told me we'd break the session into three parts. He'd lead the first part with circuit routines boiled up in a mad scientist's laboratory. I'd have part two, with my Lucha Libre expertise and free rein to reshape the Mort-tician into the wrestler of my choosing. Part three would be what Sensei called "a combined effort. "I didn't want to think about what fresh torture was in store for the Fink in that round.

Sensei chirped off his famous whistle and set the Mort-tician in motion. On each side of the ring, ropes dangled from the rafters above. Mr. Finkelstein had to climb a rope and receive the wounds of a water balloon bombing from Sensei, then climb down and crawl under the ring--which Sensei had packed full of the most obscure obstacles you could think of, like puddles of hot wax and old rakes and a whole box of stray Lego pieces which clung to my teacher's knees and elbows when he roared out the other side with his t-shirt smeared in hot candle wax. Then he shot right back up the other rope, probably welcoming the cooling relief of an exploding water balloon.

The Fink ran back and forth through this

mess for a good twenty minutes before Sensei shouted, "Get your revenge, Toby!"

I had no idea what he meant by "revenge." But I knew it was my turn to lay into the Mort-tician, so I led him to the ring. Let him catch his breath. Gave him a bit of mercy since I knew (too well) he deserved it.

"New move," I said. "The spinning head-scissors. One of the most common moves in a luchador's pocket."

"What should I do?" he asked through heavy bouts of wheezing. As luck would have it, the door to Zeke's office swung open (like I said, pretty rare) and Zeke stepped out in his designer suit with an industrial-scented cigar in hand.

"Hey Zeke, give us a hand?" I asked. It was a gutsy move because I'd never heard Zeke say more than a word or two since I first walked into his gym and, well, he was kind of enormous. Like, I'm pretty sure he can lift a thousand pounds. Give or take.

"Don't bother me, kid," he said. "I'm busy." Then he stood there in a cloud of his own cigar smoke and didn't move. Not a muscle.

I shrugged and started to show the Mort-tician the new technique. How he'd need to run right at me and then spring off his hands with just enough space between the two of us to latch his boots around my head and send me flying in the opposite direction.

The first few attempts were absolute failures. Each time, the Mort-tician looked more like a flabby bowling ball rolling into the gutters of wrestling history than a seasoned luchador capable of head-scissoring an opponent nine rows deep in the stands.

But then he got the handspring part down pretty well. Soon, could latch on and flip an opponent into any corner of the ring. The session was almost complete when I heard a voice bellow out over my shoulder.

"Alright, kid, you got me," he said.

"What?" I spun around to meet Zeke's eyes as he stepped into the ring.

"Let's see if he can handle someone his own size," Zeke said, with an evil grin rising on his lips. The kind of grin you make when you say "someone his own size" but you actually mean, "HAHAHAHAHA!"

"You want him to try the move on you?" I asked.

"Anything to help a friend," he said. Then he laughed a little which made me nervous, but also made me want to see how this would play out. I mean, Sensei did give me 'free rein' over my portion of the session sooo...

I accepted.

And then I watched Norbert M. Finkelstein bound off the far ropes, approach the mountainous Zeke with a full head of steam, hit his handspring to perfection, and...

Bounce off Zeke the way a golf ball pings off a baseball bat. The whole time Zeke stood there in his designer suit, puffing his nasty cigar, acting like he'd just been kissed by a light breeze.

That's when the coach in me was born.

When the legend of El Machina truly came to life.

It happened the second I scooped my

English teacher off the mat, steadied him against the turnbuckle and said, "Not bad."

"Not bad? Were you watching?"

"Well, it was bad," I said, "but you can build on it."

"How? Should I skip the whole ricochet part next time and explode on impact?"

"No," I said. Cool and calm. Just like that. Like an old, weathered corner man who's seen more matches than days in his life. "All you need to do is drive with your legs. Use them to pull you through the handspring and try to slam into someone who's standing behind Zeke."

"Behind him?" I nodded, and I could see his eyes glaze over for a moment as he contemplated the strategy. "I get it," he said.

And the Mort-tician sure meant it when he said it, because on the next attempt, he rushed full speed at Zeke, hit the handspring, drove his legs through the opponent, and flipped that beast halfway to El Paso!

Mr. F was polite about it, too. After clobbering his favorite gym owner, he rolled to his feet and caught the man's twirling cigar in his bare hand before it could burn a hole in the canvas.

"Not bad," Zeke said as he wobbled to his feet and snatched the cigar back from the Mort-tician. "Not bad at all."

After Zeke evaporated into his office (probably for another six-week hibernation period), Sensei popped out of the locker room like an angry prairie dog and shouted, "Final round! All out destruction!" which didn't amount to much, other than me and Sensei running the Fink through an obstacle course I wouldn't even wish on Joey Happenstance. It was fun, though. At least, for me.

What we did was borrow a bunch of tackling dummies from Coach Seam, courtesy of Mapleton Middle School Football. I set them up around the ring, and the Mort-tician had to hit them with the moves I'd taught him so far...all as Sensei bombarded him with water balloons. I swear, the man is obsessed with water balloons. I found out why a few seconds later, when he pulled his cooler full of them up beside me and said, "Bombs away!"

I mean, can you honestly say you wouldn't whip a few water balloons at your teacher if you had the chance? Yeah. I wasn't passing that up. So I fired hard and true. And the Mort-tician head-scissored, and plancha-ed, and pile drove every one of those tackling dummies as we fired balloons at him and Sensei screamed, "If we hit you, start over!"

But we never hit him. Not once. He was too fast, and he knew the moves better than I do. There was no stopping the Mort-tician in round three. So, it was a good day. I mean, is Mr. Finkelstein destined to climb the heights of Mt. Luchador and take a seat next to wrestling legends?

Probably not.

But did the Mort-tician look like a different wrestler than he did last week? I'd have to say 'yes'. Most definitely so. And, if he's not, it doesn't matter.

There's no turning back.

Monday, April 22

ALL GOOD COACHES BASE their decisions on research. In fact, most anything you do in life requires research in some form or another. At least, if you want to succeed.

Like Dad.

He never stepped in the ring without an inside-out knowledge of every kick, punch, and aerial move his opponent might use. He called it 'being prepared for the unexpected'. Most people just call it a 'scouting report'.

To learn about the unexpected before it happened, Dad would send his legendary wrestling coach, Manuel (who was just a retired fisherman from Miami), around El Paso to all the local gyms and he'd scout the talent and share the valuable intel with the one and only El Carisma Solano. Then my dad would mold his training sessions around the strengths and weaknesses of whatever unlucky soul he was set to fight that week.

The strategy worked, time and time again, in every match El Carisma ever fought until the injury.

I knew if I wanted to call myself a valuable member of Sensei Clement's training staff, I had to make myself useful. I had to dig up the facts, cross all my Is and dot all my Ts (wait, did I say that right?) on my scouting report of The Champ, and train my worthy subject (that's Mr. Finkelstein) for the precise opponent that lies ahead of him.

The only problem was The Champ trained at the Nautilus Training Center and Spa, all the way across town and definitely not within walking distance from Mapleton Middle School.

First, I did the natural thing. I asked Mom if she could give Jimmy and me a lift after practice and then wait in the parking lot while we went on a scouting mission. She looked at me with only half her face visible above a stack of ungraded tests and essays. I wasn't surprised when she said, "Does it look like I have time to drive you to the Nautilus Center for no good reason?"

I wanted to tell her creating a scouting report on The Champ was a perfectly good reason (no, a great reason!) for driving a few miles out of her way, but the frizzled hair and the bold creases in her brow told me I'd be wise not to proceed.

We couldn't ask Fink, because then he'd know Jimmy and me were trying to gain him an advantage and he'd go all ballistic on us and say something like, "Why don't you boys go home and stay out of it?" We thought about asking Sensei for a lift, but decided that was probably a risk best left to stunt car drivers and crash-test dummies. I mean, it was a matter of survival.

About the only person left to ask was Coach Seam. "Oh, sure. I'm all about it," he said about a millisecond after I asked him, which was cool because a good coach can always respect a good strategy.

After practice, I told Mom my plan and that I'd be home for dinner. Then Jimmy and I hopped in the back of Coach Seam's vehicle. On the ride from Mapleton Middle to the Nautilus, all three of us were in pretty good spirits.

Jimmy sat there in the back-seat cracking insults on The Champ like, "I'll bet he just sits in the spa sipping smoothies all day. I mean, how much training do you need to beat wrestlers like Big Baby? I'm serious!"

I was busy laughing at Jimmy's burn session, which is a whole lot funnier (but still kind of mean) when it's directed at someone other than yourself.

Even Coach Seam was excited about the recon mission. "Great idea, boys," he told us. "We should learn everything we need to know today."

And we did. About two seconds after we stepped inside the gym and saw the towering mound of muscle that was The Champ standing at center ring.

His blue mascara was strapped

firmly over his head, so all that stared back at us were his gray eyes and the tiny lightning bolt patterns stitched on the front of the mask. Heavy, white wrestling boots rose to his kneecaps, with electric blue wrestling tights tucked in the top and a thick, golden bolt of lightning crackling down each leg.

Happenstance sat at a folding table beside the ring. His fingers were covered in grease from eating sardines right from the can (which sounds totally disgusting but looked even worse). His head perked up from the can when he noticed us lurking in the shadows of the gym. He smiled and stared at us for as long as it took him to be sure we knew he knew we were there. Then he snapped his fingers and shouted something to The Champ, and The Champ nodded. That's all. He didn't say a word. Just nodded and watched three monstrous-looking sparring partners (each one bigger than the next, and all three of them bigger than Mr. Finkelstein) crawl under the ropes.

The first thing I did was look at Jimmy's face. The next thing I did was look at Coach Seam's face. I didn't need to look at my own face because I could tell my jaw was dropped open and I was probably drooling just like my fellow coaches.

Then Happenstance chucked his empty sardine can at the bell and CLANG! The practice match was on.

And then it ended.

Like, if I would have blinked one more time, I think I would have missed the whole thing. That's how quickly The Champ disposed of all three beasts in one swoop. First, he hit them with a triple clothesline while Happenstance's sardine can was still vibrating on the gym floor. Then he spent the rest of the match flying through the air, from rope to canvas to turnbuckle and back, with enough tornillos and planchas, and outright dropkicks to obliterate an entire army of wrestling superstars, let alone these three poor fools who probably didn't even get a stray sardine bone from Happenstance for their service.

To end it, The Champ piled all three woozy opponents on top of each other like wounded wrestling mats and crushed all of them at once with an epic chest splash from the top rope.

After the pin, The Champ popped to his feet without a droplet of sweat on his face, and he covered the network of tattoos up and down his back with a blue robe, and then sat in the corner of the ring to enjoy a strawberry smoothie.

"I told you!" Jimmy said.

But this time I didn't laugh, and Coach Seam didn't laugh. Neither did Jimmy, because nothing about what we'd just witnessed was funny. In fact, as we walked out of the Nautilus and hopped in Coach Seam's car, we said nothing at all. But I know what we were thinking:

Norbert M. Finkelstein is a dead man.

Friday, April 26

I HAVEN'T STOPPED THINKING about The Champ since Monday night, when Jimmy, Coach Seam, and I came to the logical conclusion that my English teacher may no longer exist after Mother's Day. That's if we can't get him to call off the challenge match. I mean, I know it sounds kind of cowardly to make the guy call off a match we had so much trouble convincing him to enter in the first place. But this was a matter of life or death...or, at least, the death of a wrestling career (which might be worse).

So, I called an emergency meeting of the only people at Mapleton Middle who know how dangerously close the Mort-tician is teetering on the edge of a cliff. That happened to be me, Jimmy, Coach Seam, and Maya (since I texted her a brief summary of our scouting trip). We met in Coach Seam's office in the basement of the gym during lunch--which should show you how terrified we are for Mr. F, because I don't skip meals for anyone.

The first five minutes of the emergency meeting was a bunch of shouting back and forth at each other, which did nothing but reinforce the fact we were all pretty sure Mr. Finkelstein would get himself killed (or, at least, severely humiliated) if he stepped in the ring with The Champ.

"Why don't we tell him to call it off?" Coach Seam asked, which seemed logical to anyone who didn't understand wrestling honor or has never met Joey Happenstance.

"He'd never go for it," I said.

"Not after how Crap-penstance embarrassed him in front of his mother," Jimmy agreed.

"Well, I don't see what the big deal is," Maya said from her seat behind Seam's desk. "The Mort-tician has fought some tough characters in the past few months. What's one more?"

"Do you hear yourself right now?" I asked.

"Tough characters? Are you talking about Big Baby?"

"Yeah," Jimmy said. "The Champ is nothing like Big Baby."

"He's nothing like any of Norbie's opponents," Coach Seam added. "In fact, he's like no wrestler I've ever seen before."

"He's basically indestructible," I told her.

"Indestructible?" she asked. Maya leaned back in Seam's desk chair and plopped her feet on the desk. "So you're saying he's not the typical MWF wrestler?"

"I'm saying he's not typical at all," I shot back. "He can probably bench press a locomotive, he's lightning fast, and his feet barely touch the mat when he fights."

"That's because he's usually clobbering people from the top ropes," Jimmy added.

"I get it, Jimmy," Maya said. "But it sure is interesting."

"What's interesting?" Coach Seam asked, pushing Maya's feet off the surface of his desk with the end of an old ruler.

"Nothing," she said. "Not yet...but I still say we should try to get the Mort-tician as prepared as we can."

"You mean, teach him enough to survive?" I asked. Maya nodded. Her glasses slid down her nose a little, and she pushed them back up the bridge. They were the same ones she always wore, not new or anything--which reminded me of something.

"I can try," I told her. Then I asked, "Didn't you say you had an eye doctor appointment today?" just to see what she would say.

"Oh...yes," Maya said. Then she got all weird and gathered up her books at warp speed. "I'm...running late." She swept past us and returned to higher ground.

"You really think you and Sensei can get Mr. Finkelstein prepared in time?" Jimmy asked when Maya was gone.

"No," I said. "I'm gonna need your help. Both of you."

That's how Jimmy, Coach Seam, and I wound up at Zeke's Gym after practice to join

Sensei's secret training battalion. Maya didn't make it, of course. Another eye appointment or something. I guess I can't blame her because I'm pretty sure 'vision' ranks above 'training session' on just about anyone's priority list.

Sensei was surprised to see the extra help show up in the forms of Jimmy and Coach Seam, but only a fraction of the amount of surprise we saw from Mr. Finkelstein. "Seam?" he asked. "What in the world are you doing here?"

"We need to bring out the big guns, Norbie. Get you prepared for the toughest match of your life."

"I thought Sensei and Toby were already doing that," Mr. F said. His hands were on his hips and his shoulders were pulled up tight to his ears, so I could tell he was losing his patience.

"It might be a tougher match than that, my friend," Coach Seam said. "We're here to help."

"Help with what?" Mr. F asked.

"We're gonna make you fly," Jimmy said, which sounded stupid at first, but on second thought was one hundred percent accurate.

We skipped Sensei's circuit-training torture today and tossed aside my personal round with the Mort-tician in favor of a no-holds-barred, combined session where all four "trainers" would attempt to teach a three-hundred pound man with limited athletic ability to float as lightly and carefree as a butterfly.

That meant I demonstrated three quick moves to the Mort-tician I'd learned from watching countless matches involving El Carisma. All of them are considered aerials, or above-the-ropes- moves, which meant big boy was going to fly, just as Jimmy had said.

The three moves were:

El Salto Mortal - "the somersault"- which was a common but dangerous
move in which the attacking luchador climbed the turnbuckle in the corner of the ring, stood facing the crowd, and then backflipped off the top rope and into a weary opponent's chest.

La Quebrada - "the broken" - which was a

pretty standard evasive technique in

the Lucha Libre world. That means it was a way to avoid getting clobbered. With an opponent charging quickly, a seasoned luchador would use quebrada to step on the middle rope and catapult up and over the opponent in a splendid backflip.

La Patada Charva - "the Charva Kick" - named after its inventor, this aerial drop kick from the top rope can wreak havoc on an opponent standing either inside or outside the ring.

I mean, I'm no El Carisma (I'm not even El Machina yet), but I performed each one of these moves on Coach Seam's tackling dummies well enough so the Mort-tician could see what we wanted him to do. And... well... this is what happened:

El Salto Floppo - "the somer-flop" - the Mort-tician climbed the turnbuckle, faced

the crowd, roared to his adoring fans, and then slipped and fell like a rock to the concrete outside the ring. It took a full jug of ice water and some smelling salts to revive him.

El Retorcido - "the twisted" - Since Jimmy was the smallest, he volunteered to

bull rush the Mort-tician from across the ring, and the Mort-tician demonstrated the exact opposite of what you'd call an 'evasive' technique when his massive foot missed the second rope and he spun over the top and back around the middle rope in the only living basketweave pattern in human history. We had to call Zeke out of his office with a pair of pliers to set the poor guy loose.

La Patada Fantasma - "the phantom kick" - Don't be fooled by the cool name in

the same way I was fooled when the Mort-tician climbed to the top rope without issue and lined up to drop kick the tackling dummy at center ring. Because that's when the door swung open and Zeke's mailman popped in with his bag full of letters. "Afternoon!" he shouted with a tip of his postal cap, and that was enough to shatter the Mort-tician's balance. He teetered to the left. To the right. He spun completely around at least three times on the top rope, and then he jumped with his front leg outstretched in perfect drop kick formation. Only problem was he totally missed the tackling dummy and he connected with the one object in the entire gymnasium that was more dangerous than all the rest: Sensei. None of us bothered to save the Mort-tician from what ensued once Sensei realized what had hit him.

So, now the Mort-tician's coaching staff is trying to decide whether to keep the training on track, or to simply contact his mom and Ms. Gluten and tell them to get a jump on the guy's funeral arrangements.

It's a tough call.

Wednesday, May 1
– May Day

TODAY WAS THE FIRST of May, which some people call 'May Day', and that's pretty much the best description I can give you about the distress call that got blasted all over Mapleton this evening.

I mean, it started out like any other day. Most of them do. I woke up, went to school, talked Mort-tician training strategy with Maya and Jimmy at lunch, and completed a highly educational season of spring (fake) wrestling with a final practice.

But then things got weird. Exciting at first...but then super weird.

What happened was, Mom showed up at the end of practice like she hasn't done in months. At first, I thought the whole Coach Seam infatuation thing was stirring up again, and I immediately felt a rush of hot sweat spill down the back of my singlet. But Mom walked right past Coach Seam without noticing he was there.

Instead, she made a beeline to Mr. Finkelstein and launched into a super-animated conversation with a ton of laughter and head bobbing. Then I distinctly saw her mouth the words, "Thank you. He'll love it."

And what she was about to tell me? She was right. I did love it, because I'd never had a chance to sit in the audience for a live radio broadcast in a real recording studio, and that was exactly what Mr. Finkelstein had offered.

Not just me, either. He invited Mom, Maya, and Jimmy too. He even invited Coach Seam, who said he couldn't make it, but he'd be listening on his drive out to visit his two daughters. Plus, I was sure Ms. Gluten would be the Fink's guest of honor, so I imagined the studio of the popular, drive-time show 'P.B. to the Max!' would be loaded down with Mapleton Middle School folk by the time the Mort-tician hit the airwaves.

So, that was the exciting part of the day.

Mom had agreed to swing by Jimmy's and Maya's houses on the way and give them a lift to the show. We all piled into our seats in Recording Studio B and enjoyed five minutes of awesomeness as spotlights flickered and danced across the radio panel, spectators filed in, and the excitement built to a fevered pitch.

That's when the weird part of the day began. And I mean 'weird' as in totally catastrophic for the Mort-tician. The whole thing started out pretty well, but then something unexpected happened--something none of us could have foreseen--that left us wanting to scream, "Mayday! Mayday!" instead of simply observing May Day. Here's how the broadcast unfolded:

The house lights flickered and went dark, and two dueling spotlights whirled around the crowd as the cheesiest theme music you ever heard played in the background. The spotlights settled on the sound board at center stage, and the house announcer said with his voice drenched in bass, "Annnnd NOW! Your host of

PB to the MAX! The loveable... the hilarious... the favorite son of Mapleton... MisssssTER P...... B........ Serviccccce!" Then a sign flashed above the stage that read 'Applause!' and everyone in the seats around me started clapping as if P.B. Service was their favorite person in the world.

P.B. sat down and started the show by talking about the MWF and the "winding road his next guest has walked through its ranks." Then he was like, "Please welcome, the MORT-TICIAN!" And Mr. Finkelstein wobbled out from backstage in his frilly suit and his ridiculous mascara with the 'Applause!' sign flashing at an inhuman rate.

P.B. started the interview and, for the first time, the Fink actually looked and sounded somewhat comfortable. No fumbling over words. No quiver in his voice. Nothing at all resembling the strange, gurgling noises he made on his last trip to the show, way back when I still lived in El Paso. P.B. leaned in close to his microphone and asked the

Mort-tician, "What is it that makes you think you're ready for a match with The Champ?" and Mr. Finkelstein stared directly at him through the crude cutouts in his mask and said with cool confidence, "I'm ready."

That's when the studio doors swung open and the whole place was blinded by the light rushing in from the lobby. When my eyes adjusted, there were two wrestlers and P.B. seated on the stage...and only one of them was my English teacher. The other wore a blue mascara with lightning bolts embroidered under the eyes. "My goodness!" P.B. shouted in the least believable expression of surprise I'd ever heard in my life. "The Champ, everyone!" and the spotlights cruised around the audience again. The cheesy theme music rose and fell, and the 'Applause!' sign flashed a mile a minute. It was clear the Mort-tician had been set up for this very moment so that good, old P.B. could keep his listeners--all irritated drivers sitting in traffic--from turning the dial.

The interview continued, though at this

point I wouldn't call it an interview as much as I'd call it a verbal beat-down of the highest order. And every ounce of it came crashing down on the Mort-tician's back. The Champ walked over to P.B.'s chair, grabbed it by the backrest, and then rolled the snivelling pipsqueak right out of the studio in one, monstrous heave. First came the clatter of equipment from stage left, where P.B. came to rest, then the 'Applause!' signs flashed like crazy, and then The Champ grabbed hold of P.B.'s microphone. He swung it around to within an inch of Fink's face and leaned in as close as he could get to the Mort-tician without physically gobbling off his nose. And then he just stood there staring down at him. In total silence. I mean, he didn't say a single word. There was just the gasp of the audience, the creaking of the Mort-tician's swivel chair as he shrank down in it to the size of a silver dollar pancake, and complete and total dead air in every car on the highway that was tuned to WYMP FM.

After two full minutes of the silent and

deadly stare down from The Champ, and another thirty seconds of Mr. Finkelstein's strained whimpering filtering out over the airwaves, the cheesy theme music kicked back up, the house announcer said, "We'll be right back after a message from our sponsors. Don't go anywhere!" and the Mapleton Middle School faithful (that's us) slinked out of the studio before anyone could identify us.

So, that could have probably went better in the lead-up to the Mort-tician's biggest match against an opponent he has no chance of beating or even surviving. Which leaves me with only one more thing left to say:

"Mayday! Mayday!"

Monday, May 6

YESTERDAY WAS CINCO DE MAYO, which was perfect because it gave me a good reason to forget about the challenge match for awhile, and about the Mort-tician's inevitable destruction at the hands of The Champ, and about my failures as a newbie wrestling trainer. Instead, I was able to focus on my family (which is just me and Mom now) and my culture (which will connect me and Dad forever).

It's kind of sad how Cinco De Mayo has morphed into this day in the United States where people think it's time to celebrate Mexican salsa or something. Cinco De Mayo is so much more important than a few stale chips at a chain restaurant. It marks the date (way back in 1862) when the Mexican army defeated their French oppressors at the Battle of Puebla. Dad and I loved to talk about the victory. How it was more inspirational than strategic because it was the first time the Mexican people demonstrated how tired they were of getting bullied by Napoleon's army, and they fought against all odds to defend the land that was rightfully their own.

It was also kind of sad that Dad wasn't here in Mapleton to celebrate with Mom and me. To sit around the table and feast on Mom's best dishes--her mole poblano sauce slathered on roast pork, and her famous chalupas poblanas, and I couldn't forget her chiles en nogada all sprinkled in sesame seeds.

And Dad would lean back in his chair and recount war stories from Mexico's great past that had happened over a century before my father was even born, and we'd be happy. Just the three of us. Together on a day we could celebrate being who we are and being a family.

I still ate all of Mom's food this year despite Dad's absence (I mean, I'm not stupid), but not having him here meant a crucial ingredient was missing from our traditional Cinco feast. So I can't say the food tasted the same here in Mapleton as it did back in El Paso.

None of that mattered at lunch today. Not here in a town where Toby and Cait Solano were probably the only two people celebrating much of anything yesterday. Least of all was Maya, who plopped her tray down between mine and Jimmy's and proceeded to stare straight off into the great beyond, as if her brain had been siphoned out of her skull by a revolting space lizard.

"What's wrong with you?" I asked right away, because I started to get this feeling Maya's trance routine was meant to spark this very question.

She came back to life in an instant, and her eyes focused on mine through her thick lenses. "You know how I've been kind of M-I-A lately?" she asked.

"Yeah," Jimmy said. "Thanks for leaving us with all the heavy lifting."

"You're welcome," Maya said to Jimmy. "Because I was lifting a few things myself."

"Like what?" I asked.

"Pages," she told me. "Pages and pages of research." A sly smile wrinkled her lips, like she knew something neither Jimmy nor I could fathom in our lifetimes, and then she took a bite of her ham and cheese sandwich. Didn't say another word.

"And why would we care about one of your stupid school research projects?" Jimmy asked, taking Maya's silence as bait.

"Because it involves you," she said. "All of us, really. And especially the Mort-tician."

"Is that so?" I asked. "We're supposed to believe you've been sneaking around Mapleton like a private detective and uncovering secrets about our English teacher without anyone--not even your closest friends--noticing?" She didn't say anything. She just winked at me through her glasses and took another bite of her sandwich, and I knew I shouldn't have doubted her. "Okay," I said, "what did you find?"

"First of all, let me begin by saying I do not 'sneak' around. I simply follow the channels of information where they may lead."

"So you talked to Ms. Gluten?" Jimmy asked.

"I talked to Ms. Gluten," Maya said.

"And she pointed you in the right direction?" I asked.

"And she pointed me in the right direction," Maya repeated. "Only this time, the right direction wasn't so obvious. This time I needed both my curiosity and some blind luck to get me where I needed to go."

"And where would that be?" Jimmy asked, his tongue loaded with skepticism.

"Billington's Comic Shop."

"That crappy little place on Orchard Avenue?" I asked.

"The one that's had a going-out-of-business sale for the past two years?" Jimmy asked.

"The same," Maya told him. "I know it sounds weird, but hear me out. It all started last week after you went to scout The Champ."

"Total disaster," I said.

"Not totally," Maya corrected. "Sure, you found out The Champ is basically indestructible and that he'll most likely carve Mr. Finkelstein down into bite-sized Mort-tician nuggets when they fight."

"How is that not a total loss?" Jimmy asked.

"Didn't you wonder why The Champ is so indestructible? Why he's so much more talented than the other wrestlers in the MWF?" Jimmy and I looked at each other. The eyebrow above his left eye raised a notch or two. "Well, I wanted to know," Maya continued, "so that's when I brought Ms. Gluten into it."

"Why didn't you just ask Ms. Gluten to talk the Fink out of fighting the guy?" Jimmy asked.

"I did," Maya said. "And she tried, but Mr. Finkelstein wouldn't listen to her, so I thought a new plan of attack was in order."

"So, what did you find?" I asked. "I mean, out with it already!"

Maya sighed, as if speedy delivery and the research process clashed hard enough to make her puke. "I searched for and read everything I could about the MWF, about new wrestlers in the Mapleton area, about Joey Happenstance, and really about anything wrestling-related I could get my hands on."

"And what did you find?" I asked again, beginning to seriously lose my patience.

"Nothing," she said. "At first. But then we went to the radio show and something slapped me square in the face. It happened when The Champ burst through the doors and all those weird spotlights were bouncing off him. That's when I saw it."

"Oh my God! What did you see?" I shouted, and a few heads popped up to gawk at us from the surrounding tables.

"His tattoo," Maya said.

"A tattoo?" Jimmy asked. "So what? There are too many tattooed wrestlers in the world to count."

"But not many with this particular tattoo on his back," Maya said. "In fact, there's only one. Have a look. I came across this down at Billington's Comics, in the back of an old wrestling fanzine that was on sale for forty-eight cents."

Her reasoning became clear as soon as I glanced at the page. It stared me right in the face and said, "Yes, Toby. That's right. It's me!"

And it was. Him. The baddest, meanest, most ruthless rudo ever to don the mascara of a luchador. It was El Ciclon. The Tornado. The one and only. The man who'd destroyed my father and my family with a single aerial move. An outlawed move. The "tabletop tornillo". Where only a deceitful and dishonorable rudo could haul a foreign object--a folding table--into the ring, place his opponent on its face, and then punish him through it with a twisting, cyclonic elbow drop from the top rope. He turned my father's knee to confetti with that move, and with it El Carisma's career. I could never forgive a man for such a deed, but I wasn't sure why Maya had forced me to look at this page she'd uncovered which featured the mighty Jorge 'El Ciclon' Rodriguez in his trademark mascara with tornados instead of lightning bolts under the eyes, as he growled at the crowd.

"What is this?" I asked Maya.

"Don't you recognize him?" she asked. "He's the guy who--"

"I know who he is," I said, "but why am I looking at him?"

She pulled another picture out of her pocket, this one clipped from a piece *El Rey* of newsprint. "I found this shot at the county library," she said. "It's the only one that shows his back." She laid it down on the table and I saw it immediately. The tattoo. The one we'd all seen during our scouting trip to the Nautilus and at his match against Big Baby. The one that read "El Rey" in bold, script letters.

Everything had become crystal clear. The Champ wasn't just the champion of the MWF. The Champ--the same guy we'd carelessly pushed our poor English teacher into challenging for the title--was none other than the dreaded El Ciclon! But that still left one question.

"I don't get it," I said to Maya. "Why here? Why Mapleton? I mean, this guy was a wrestling superstar when I left El Paso."

"Good question," Maya said. "I had Ms. Gluten do a bit more digging, and she found out El Ciclon was banned from wrestling."

"Because of what he did to my father?"

"No," Maya said. "Unfortunately not. It had something to do with him pulling another wrestler's mask off or something."

"You mean he unmasked another luchador?"

"Sounds like it," Maya said. I knew that the only thing more dishonorable than deliberately trying to injure other luchadors with illegal moves, was unmasking a fellow wrestler in the ring and revealing that wrestler's true identity-- thus erasing a luchador completely from history.

"Unmasking?" Jimmy asked. "What does this all mean for us?"

"It means there's no way The Champ is a legal wrestler in the MWF," Maya said. "All we have to do is alert the officials to his true identity and the match is off. The Mort-tician will live to fight another day."

"That's great!" Jimmy shouted.

"Except it's not," I said. "We can't turn The Champ in to MWF officials."

"What are you talking about, Toby? Of course we can," Maya said.

"Not if we don't want to be just like him," I told them.

"You're not making any sense," Maya said. "This is life and death we're talking about."

"We can't unmask him, Maya," I said. "That goes against the code, and we didn't come this far to go and get the wrestling gods all mad at us."

"You and your stupid wrestling gods, Toby! I swear--"

"He's right," Jimmy said. "We need to do this the right way. Within the rules and within the code. Even if that seems almost impossible at this point."

"Almost impossible?" Maya asked. "Try definitely and totally impossible. Come on, this is no time to mess around with old codes and wrestling gods when we--"

"Don't worry," I said. "There might be another way. I think I have a plan."

"You do?" Maya asked, sounding genuinely surprised.

"Totally," I said.

"And what is it?" Jimmy asked.

"I said don't worry, didn't I? The wheels are already in motion."

And that seemed enough to set Jimmy's and Maya's worries to rest. At least, for now.

Wednesday, May 8

I'VE SPENT EVERY SECOND since Monday's El Ciclon revelation at lunch trying to figure out the plan I told Maya and Jimmy I already had in place. Spoiler alert: I don't have a plan in place. I just didn't want my friends to feel totally defeated knowing their English teacher was set to fight one of the most brutal and ruthless *rudos* I'd ever seen wrestle with my own eyes.

I mean, the way I see it, once the bell rings on Sunday afternoon, the Mort-tician has about ten seconds to straight-up run away before El Ciclon (cough, cough The Champ) compresses him into a human basketball and dribbles him around the ring. It won't be pretty, and the last thing I want for Mr. Finkelstein is for him to get the El Carisma treatment—out of luck, out of wrestling, and out of my life.

But I had no plan. Not even the tiniest fiber

of a thread that could eventually be woven into something that resembled a plan. It was clear the Mort-tician would never back down at this point. It was much too late for that, and the man's honor was at stake. I mean, technically, he was the one who issued the challenge (with prodding from some students I won't name). How would it look in Mapleton if the Fink got humiliated over the airwaves and then pulled out of the match all in the course of a few days? Not good, I can tell you that. He'd be a laughingstock. No, worse than a laughingstock. He'd be a Big Baby, and I couldn't allow my sweet, innocent English teacher to walk down that lonely path.

So, I was at a loss. It almost came to the point where I was ready to call up Jimmy and Maya and confess to them I had no plan at all, and we should just stash Mr. Finkelstein in witness protection or something and flee the country with the small shreds of dignity we still had intact.

I never wished Dad were here more than

now. I could tell him anything and he'd never make me feel like an idiot for asking his advice, no matter how dumb my questions proved to be. And he'd always know what to do. One hundred percent of the time. Yes, El Carisma would know what to do, especially when it came to Ciclon (his arch nemesis).

And then I was like, "Wait a minute!" I mean, it hit me so hard I literally said the words out loud. Wasn't Dad the same old guy he's always been even if he's a few thousand miles away? Even though I haven't spoken to him in months?

I remembered what Mom said when she slipped me the piece of paper with Dad's new phone number on it. "You can talk to him whenever you want." Or, I guess, whenever I was ready.

Tonight, I reached the point where I can finally say I was ready to talk to Carlos Solano, and to begin treating him like my father again. So I sent him this text: DAD, I THINK I NEED UR HELP. Less than a minute later he responded with: ANYTHING.

And that, my friends, is how a plan is hatched.

Sunday, May 12

– Mother's Day (and the big match)

TODAY WAS MOTHER'S DAY. The day of the big match. I made sure to buy Mom a big bouquet of sunflowers (her favorite!) and had them in a vase full of water on the kitchen table when she came down to make breakfast in the morning. But breakfast had already been made!

It was an El Machina special I whipped up by reading the backs of boxes and following the directions to a tee—which netted me one, fully-formed pancake that I shoveled onto Mom's plate and slathered in butter. I probably wouldn't have eaten the thing myself, but Mom seemed to love the misshapen flapjack and the side of sunflowers.

"These were the same ones your dad used to

buy me at that little flower shop in El Paso!" she told me, brushing her hand through the long, yellow petals. I already knew this fact, of course (more on that later), but it was still cool to get a big hug and feel Mom's happy tears on the back of my neck.

I have to admit, it was a pretty good gift. But it wasn't even the best gift of the day. Not by a longshot! Those gifts were all handed out at Mapleton Auditorium, site of the Sunday Cavalcade of MWF Wrestling which happened to feature a title match between The Champ and his challenger, one Norbert M. Finkelstein.

I don't want to waste any time here. I'll get directly to the match, because it was a thing of beauty and I was pleasantly surprised by the results (see: Mr. Finkelstein managed to survive intact).

Here's how it all went down:

First, the whole auditorium filled up with fans until it became a tumultuous sea of waving hands and flashy masks and homemade signs. Until the whole place vibrated under the weight of ten thousand voices. Until the popcorn vendors and the stadium ushers were lost among the swirling waves. Until an unlikely group of Mapleton Middle Schoolers filed into Mort-tician's Row all dressed in identical, frilly suit jackets with the sleeves torn off and novelty mascaras over their heads.

That's when the spotlight fell on center ring, and the ring announcer stepped out and took hold of her great, big microphone in the sky and said, "Ladies and gentlemen! Welcome to the Sunnnnnnnnnnnnn-DAY Caval-CADE!" The whole place went bananas, nearly rocking the poor Mapleton Auditorium off its foundation. "And in tonight's main event," she continued, "a title match between The Champ and his challenger...THEEEE...Morrrrrrrrrr-TICIAN!"

A bunch of pyrotechnics blasted off in front of the tunnel, and the Mort-tician burst through the resulting sparks and smoke and bounded toward the ring at a speed neither I nor Sensei had ever witnessed during any of our training sessions. The crowd was largely silent, except for one particular section of the Fink's superfans who happened to be sitting ringside.

"Go Norbie!" Ms. Gluten shouted from the row behind me.

"Kick his butt, Mort-tician!" Jimmy shouted in the seat to my left.

Even Mom got into the Mort-tician spirit, shouting, "No mercy!" over and over again from about two inches away from my eardrums.

The Mort-tician reached the ring and, in one quick motion, propelled himself up and over the ropes like a jackrabbit. His arms rippled out of the holes in his suit jacket like twin telephone poles if they were made from chiseled granite, and he hopped from one foot back to the other so lightly it almost looked like he was capable of floating across the canvas. I mean, the dude had totally transformed from a middle school English teacher into a physical specimen in the few days since our last training session.

And I wasn't the only one to notice.

My eyes panned down to The Champ's

corner, where that slimy, no-good Joey Happenstance stood sentry waiting for his illegal wrestler to emerge from the locker room. His eyes popped out of his head at the sight of the new Norbie, something I'd figured into the equation. Something I almost kind of scripted.

So I gave Jimmy the nod, and he nodded back. I knew we'd be close to ringside, but I wasn't quite sure of Jimmy's range.

Note: I shouldn't have doubted Jimmy for a second.

Because the ace bubblegum flinger reached under his novelty mascara, pulled out the biggest, wettest, stickiest, and most disgusting-looking wad of chewed bubblegum I'd ever seen in my life. Maybe the only one of its kind in the history of bubblegum. And that young man reared back and flung the bubblegum wad a full thirty feet, over rows of cheering and unsuspecting spectators, across a cement gangway in front of the ring, and right into the curly and accepting strands of Joey's mullet. A direct hit!

And that ended Joey's fixation on the Mortician's new physique rather quickly. In fact, as the ring announcer said, "And your MWF champion...THEEEEEE CHAMMMMMP!" and as the whole place exploded in cheers for an illegitimate scoundrel of a wrestler, the only thing I and Jimmy and Maya could do was laugh hysterically because Happenstance rushed right past his own wrestler with his hand clamped down on the back of his head shouting, "Ice! Somebody get me some ice!"

With any possibility of a Happenstance protest taken care of, it was all up to the Mortician in the ring. And, for the first time since our disastrous scouting expedition, I had no doubt he'd be able to handle himself against The Champ. And, boy, was I right.

The bell rang, and The Champ puffed out his massive chest and flexed his back muscles to the crowd so the letters in his "El Rey" tattoo rippled and slithered like snakes. It was the worst move he ever made in his wrestling career. Maybe in his entire life, because that's all it took--that one millisecond where The Champ let his guard down, where he underestimated his opponent--for the Mort-tician to pounce on him.

First, it was a clothesline that almost cut El Ciclon in two, toppling him to the canvas before he could swivel his head back from the crowd and stare down his opponent through the slits in his blue mask. Then the Mort-tician went full luchador on him.

It was time for the ropes routine to come into play. The Mort-tician blasted off the far ropes at full speed and punished El Ciclon with a flying plancha to the ribs. Then he popped up and hit the ropes on the other side of the ring and consumed El Ciclon with a devastating chest splash. Then the Mort-tician scraped the groggy, half-conscious champion off the canvas and propped him against the turnbuckle, before whipping him diagonally across the ring and into a massive and painful-looking collision with the opposite turnbuckle.

The Mort-tician was all over him. Mort-tician's Row was an explosion of shouts and cheers. Happenstance was last seen at his local salon. And the title belt sat sparkling on the scorer's table. Waiting to be claimed.

The Mort-tician dragged El Ciclon to the center of the ring and lifted him off the canvas into perfect suplex formation. All he had to do was drop backward and let the chips that were El Ciclon fall where they may.

But you don't get to become a certified wrestling superstar (even in secret) without having a million tricks hidden under the old mascara. You don't get to the top without knowing how to counter--which El Ciclon did by rolling off the Mort-tician's back, sneaking up behind him, and power slamming him to the mat before the poor guy realized El Ciclon had even escaped his grip.

Mort-tician's Row got quiet in an instant. The rest of the auditorium erupted in excitement. El Ciclon hit the Mort-tician with a whole battery of his most lethal moves. From ordinary planchas to reverse centons to brutal, face-first topes. From outside the ring and from above the ropes and even with power moves that pounded the Mort-tician flat against the canvas.

He was down, and I was sure he was out. And as I stood there in my third row seat, in the heart of Mort-tician's Row, with my shoulders sagged down and the tears welling up under my novelty mascara; and as the dreaded El Ciclon, disguised as your current MWF champion, climbed to the top rope and steadied himself for a liftoff and then a crash-landing at the site of my current English teacher...

Something happened.

Something so quick and discreet that I doubt any one of those ten thousand spectators tonight caught it.

What happened was I made contact. With the Mort-tician. From my third-row seat. My eyes locked on his for just a second, and I could tell he was looking directly at me. Because he winked. And I winked back.

And that's the precise moment El Ciclon

blasted off from the top rope, and twisted through the air in his trademark, tornillo formation, and came crashing down on nothing but a blank stretch of unoccupied canvas.

The Mort-tician could counter, too.

Like I said...you don't become a wrestling superstar.

Anyway, that's when the Mort-tician decided to stop toying with the so-called champion. That's when he hit him with a leg drop. Then four more leg drops, followed by a good luck leg drop just for good measure.

The Champ gasped for air on the canvas. The hush of the crowd cut off like a faucet.

The Mort-tician climbed the turnbuckle. He pointed to Mort-tician's Row. He stared down at me and at Mom, the same way my Dad used to. Then he lifted off into a textbook tornillo and splashed down on El Ciclon like a raging tsunami.

The auditorium fell silent, but for a single row of voices. The Mort-tician scooped the Champ's legs into a cradle pin. The referee pounded the mat three times, and it was over.

The Mort-tician had defeated The Champ! He had dethroned the dreaded El Ciclon to reclaim his title, and he restored the integrity of the MWF without unmasking a fellow luchador. He'd done it all, and me and Mom and the whole town of Mapleton had been there to see it.

I ripped off my mask as the confetti washed over the crowd. And Maya ripped off her mask beside me. And then Jimmy and Mom and Coach Seam and Ms. Gluten ripped off their masks. And then a tall, roundish fellow who'd been sitting beside Ms. Gluten the entire match ripped off his mask.

"Norbie?" Ms. Gluten screeched when she saw the man's face. Coach Seam rubbed his eyes and Mom's eyes were almost popped out of her head. Maya, Jimmy, and I were less surprised. I mean, we had a plan all along.

"Shhhhh!" Mr. Finkelstein said with an index finger pushed across his grin.

"What are you doing here?" Ms. Gluten

asked.

"More importantly," Coach Seam said, "if you're out here, then who is--" Mr. Finkelstein never got to answer Coach Seam's question. Neither did Maya or Jimmy or the one and only El Machina. We didn't need to, because that's when the ring announcer carried the heavyweight belt to the center of the ring. She reached for the microphone as it drifted down from the rafters on its mile-long cord. "Your NEW...MWF Champion...THEEEEEE Mor-TICIAN!"

The Mort-tician accepted the belt that was rightfully due to him. The one he'd always deserved, and then he stepped to the edge of the canvas with flash bulbs popping all around and gazed down at the most important spectator in the auditorium at that moment: one, Cait Solano.

The Mort-tician reached inside the jacket pocket of his frilly suit and pulled out a single flower. A sunflower as gold and glowing as the belt around his waist. And that's when Cait Solano, my mom, knew exactly who was under the Mort-tician's mask. That's when every drop of Mort-tician's Row spilled into the ring, and when Carlos "El Carisma" Solano hoisted his son up on his shoulders and wrapped his arms around his wife for the first time in months. That's when I stopped thinking about my past life in El Paso and started thinking more about my future here in Mapleton. With my team and my friends and my own personal Sensei. And my family. All of it, now that Dad is staying.

I mean, what did you expect? There's not much point in having a new, improved Mort-tician around here if he can't be El Carisma.

And, don't worry. The Fink doesn't mind. He told me, and I quote, "A sundae at Jerry's with Valerie beats a Sunday of torture with Sensei any day of the week." Then he told me to write that down and carry it around with me because it may be useful someday, so I'm pretty sure he's cool with the retirement thing.

I hope he'll have time to visit Zeke's Gym

once in awhile, because those water balloons aren't going to throw themselves, and my dad isn't your typical moving target.

Not even for Sensei.

Acknowledgments:

When a book comes to life, there is literally a list of people who contributed to its creation. I am just the author. I only have so many powers, and most of those powers are simply channeled through me from the energy I gather from all of you. That is why I need to thank everyone out there who, in the past, has ever read one of my short stories, my novels, the terrible poetry I have hidden away in a box somewhere, even a new and unpolished idea I may have scribbled out on napkin one day while scarfing down Krispy Kremes. You all gave my odd and distorted brainwaves a purpose and, whether you knew it or not at the time, your encouragement inspired me to continue pushing forward on this scarred battlefield we know as the literary world.

This list certainly includes my wonderful muse and the illustrator of this novel, Alexandra Frey, who has endured the late nights, the overloaded schedules, and the unpredictable mood swings of a starving author (that's me!) for almost twenty long years while somehow making all those years feel like twenty seconds on a stopwatch. I treasure your creativity, your vision, and most of all, your patience.

The list also includes Jana Grissom and the folks at INtense Publications, who believed in the first novel in this series and urged me to revive it and continue adding to the story. Without you all, Toby Solano never comes to life.

And it includes my family, the people who never stopped believing in me when I decided to cash in my pre-med major in college for a life spent reading books, teaching writing, and being poor. Like me, you believed that money is not the root of happiness. We were right. Finally, I have to thank every student who has ever stepped foot in my classroom. You may not know it, but the inspiration you provide me on a daily basis saved my life and made me a better person...the kind of person I've always wanted to be. Thank you. Thank you. And thank you again.

About the Author:

Frank Morelli is the author of the young adult novel, *No Sad Songs* (2018), a YALSA Quick Picks for Reluctant Readers nominee and winner of an American Fiction Award for best coming of age story. The first book in his debut middle grade series, *Please Return To: Norbert M. Finkelstein* (2019), provides young readers with a roadmap to end bullying. His fiction and essays have appeared in various publications including *The Saturday Evening Post, Cobalt Review, Philadelphia Stories,* and *Jersey Devil Press.*

A Philadelphia native, Morelli's life was transformed when he accepted a teaching fellowship in the NYC Public Schools and discovered that a lifetime spent eating cafeteria tater tots would be a small price to pay for a chance to shape the future. He continues to split time between the page and the classroom, and will forever be amazed by how one enriches the other. Morelli now resides in High Point, NC with a brilliant illustrator and his three fur babies.

Connect with him on Twitter @frankmoewriter and on Instagram @frankmorelliauthor.

Read on for an exclusive extract from the
adventurous follow-up to

PLEASE RETURN TO: Toby Solano

Friday, May 31
— The Last Day of School

DEAR FELLOW INMATE OF Locker 219,

I'm sorry about all the crickets (don't ask), but I thought I'd leave you with a parting gift to make up for all the creepy crawlies.

This journal.

I know it's not much, but you may find it useful. I don't think I need it anymore, but as you make your way into middle school and into Mr. Finkelstein's class, you may benefit from understanding a bit of the history behind this journal, your teacher, the MWF, and Mapleton in general.

Who knows? You may even find it helps to add your own useless thoughts and scribbles to these withered, old pages just as I did. Just remember, whomever you turn out to be, that we're not far away. We'll be on the next hallway. In seventh grade. And at wrestling practice. And Zeke's Gym.

I can't tell you everything you'll need to know to get through the year, but I can tell you one thing for sure: we'll need you next year (which, I guess, is actually *this* year if you're just finding this letter), because I doubt Joey Happenstance will take this latest defeat sitting down. Trust me, you'll learn all about him if you do the required reading (this book, genius).

Who. Ever. U. R.

Your Future Friend,

El Machina

(AKA: Toby Solano)

CPSIA information can be obtained
at www.ICGtesting.com
Printed in the USA
FSHW011530040320
67804FS